Telephone: 01-340 3343

HIGHGATE LITERARY & SCIENTIFIC INSTITUTION
11 SOUTH GROVE N6 6BS

Time allowed 21 days

22285

Date Issued	Date Issued	Date Issued
11 JAN 1995		

Highgate Literary & Scientific Institution

B12224

BARTONWOOD

The hero of John Moat's first children's novel is a boy with a gift for riddles. Supported by his odd allies—an Infanta, a sea changeling, a Viking, and the mysterious Nossno—he fights with a clan of evil farmers, and against their weird dogs and chain-saws, for the freedom of the wood. Significantly, the story reaches its haunting showdown on Christmas Eve.

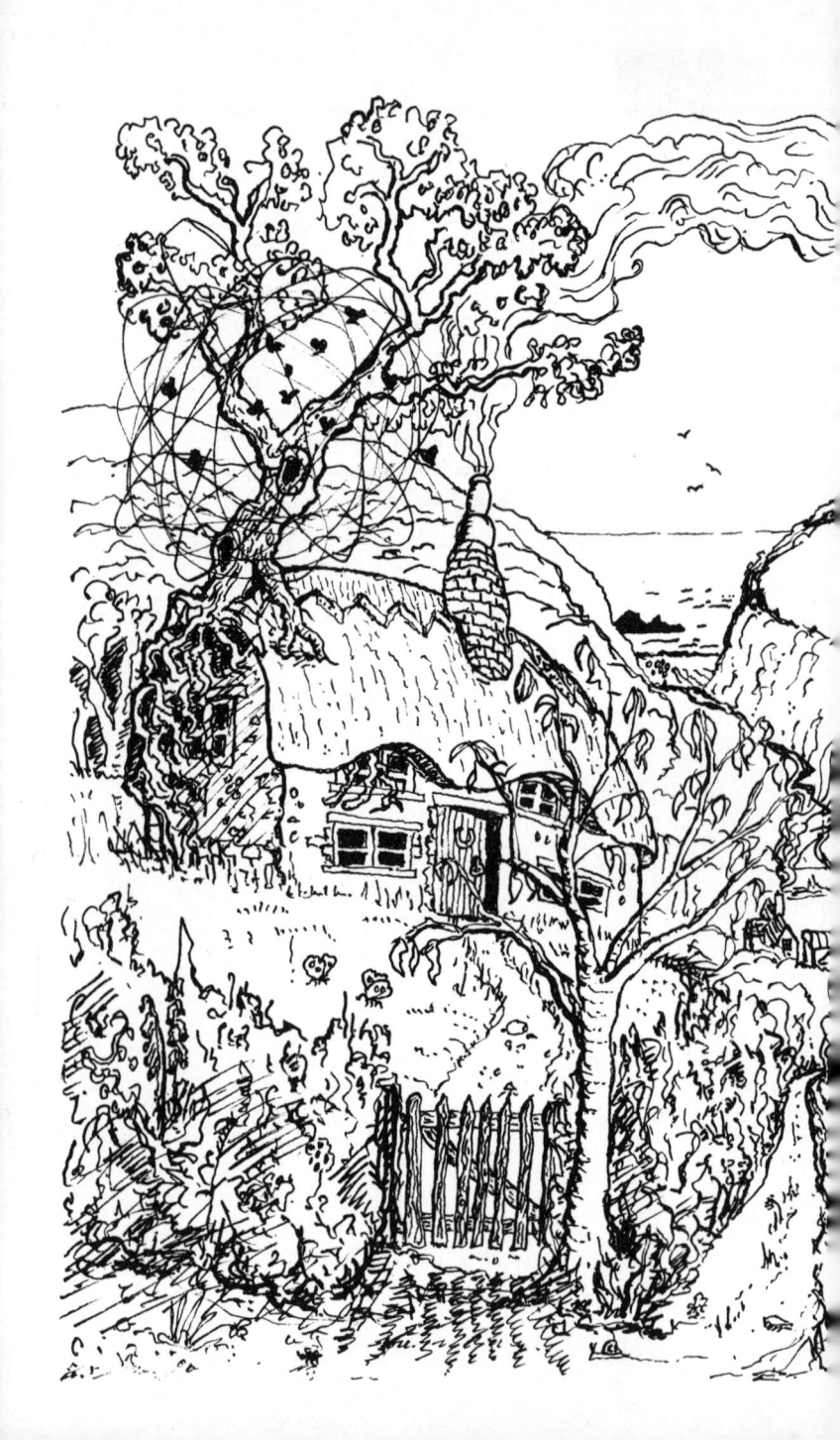

BARTONWOOD

John Moat

Illustrations by the Author

22285

Highgate
Literary & Scientific
Institution

1978
CHATTO & WINDUS · LONDON

Published by
Chatto & Windus Ltd
40-42 William IV Street
London WC2N 4DF

*

Clarke, Irwin & Co. Ltd
Toronto

British Library Cataloguing in Publication Data

Moat, John
  Bartonwood.
  I. Title
  823' .9' 1J   PZ7.M/

ISBN 0-7011-2312-5

© John Moat 1978

All rights reserved. No part of this publication
may be reproduced, stored in a retrieval system,
or transmitted, in any form, or by any means,
electronic, mechanical, photocopying, recording
or otherwise, without the prior permission of
Chatto & Windus Ltd.

Printed and bound in Great Britain by
Redwood Burn Limited
Trowbridge & Esher

Firstly, for Elsbeth and Ben, since they'll *have* to read it. Then for Sarah and Katey, Suna and Mark and Laura, whom I neglect, but have never forgotten. Also in memory of my other godson, Tom, who just might have enjoyed the book more than anyone else.

And finally for absolutely anyone who will do me the favour of writing his/her name here:

CONTENTS

Glossary	9
Spring	13
Summer	37
Autumn	63
Winter	89

FOUR QUARTERS

Spring

The wind has moved West
It shifted last night
I woke this morning
The garden was white
The raven last evening
Called winter home
But this morning the blackbird
And he was gone.

Summer

The wind has gone South
I don't recall when
I slept one moment
The garden turned green
The blackbird last evening
Sang it was spring
But this morning the cuckoo
And he was gone.

Autumn

The wind has moved East
The year's growing old
I caught her whisper
The garden turned gold
The cuckoo last evening
Called summer in
But this morning the robin
And he was gone.

Winter

The wind has moved North
Its teeth are laid bare
I searched the garden
Found nobody there
The robin last evening
Cheeped autumn's song
But this morning the raven
And he has gone.

GLOSSARY OF NAMES AND ODD WORDS

Breknis It means simply, breakfast.

Buttonsson Buttonsson's father was Peter Button (see page 14). Buttonsson's own name had been, to start with, James Button. But when he was six or seven Rustass had begun to read him some of his (Rustass's) favourite stories which were called Norse Sagas, and these were mostly about men with names like Sigurdsson and Olafsson and Thorkel Eyjolfsson. So Peter Button's son decided he'd be called Buttonsson.

Cattatoupek It isn't easy to tell how Cattatoupek got his name. It seems unlikely he was anything but distantly related to Kohoutek, the comet which a few years ago we were all told to look out for around Christmas, and which in the end was, to be quite honest, a bit of a damp squib.

Figgy-pudden That's the Bartons' Christmas pudding.

Gin avore'm is a way of saying, "Get on in front of them." Usually it tells the dog that the cows (Myrtle and Maxicrop more than likely) are heading the wrong way. It's pronounced like the sound of a diesel engine starting.

Gurt Great.

Longcripple That's a snake—maybe a cripple because of what God did to the snake in the Garden of Eden.

Muggettee Muggets are entrails, but muggettee just means glum.

Nossno When Rustass asked Buttonsson how Nossno got his name, Buttonsson said, "That would be telling." "Well, how's it spelt?" Rustass asked. "I.T." said Buttonsson. "No, Nossno," said Rustass, wearily. So Buttonsson wrote Nossno for him, only he wrote it like this, ИOSSИO . Which just could have been some sort of hint.

Peg Far as Farmer Barton's concerned, a pig's a peg.

Puttyboy On any good wrecking coast there are washed up from time to time these great globs of tallow, which seem to attract and then cling onto a whole variety of stuff: feathers, bits of net, pebbles and crabs' claws—rather in the manner of a tar-baby. Puttyboy is an excellent name for such a glob, if for no other reason because in some lights tallow can look a bit like putty. But of course there *is* another reason. Good riddle.

Rustass (Michael Rustass) There seems to be some confusion about the pronunciation of Rustass. The end *isn't* pronounced like the -ass in cutlass, still less like the -ass in molasses; it's more like the -us in Rustass, only with less weight. So put the weight on the *Rust*, and then imagine that the word rhymes with lettuce, and you'll have it about right. Important point.

Strong-tooth Ancient Norse warriors had pet weapons (swords and axes) rather as other people have pet dogs. They'd work very hard thinking up exactly the right names for the weapons (and for their ships, for that matter, see Wolf-fang-raider, page 74) because if the weapons didn't like their names they'd be almost bound to break at the wrong moment. Old swords were thought the best, because there was always a chance they'd been made by Woden or Odin. Strong-tooth must have been an old sword because those were the ones that generally gleamed when danger was near. The very best were the very oldest—these were the ones that crowed after a great victory.

Thickee Just a thick way of saying this.

Thick-wan'll larn you, bwoy. This means, "This one will teach you, boy." Or, in other words, "A gurt whisterpoop."

Tiddy-pasty A tiddy-pasty is a potato-pasty, which is potato in pastry. A Barton would eat several dozen of these in any normal week. Very filling.

Whale-road Norse warriors, when they weren't thinking up names for their swords, would often cast around for something else that could do with a new name. Whale-road was somebody's new name for the sea.

Winter-Hwen Winter-Hwen was probably to start with just a small bit left behind from a Norse saga. Still, it is important to pronounce his name correctly. Winter-Herwhén. If that's too difficult Winter-When *will* do.

Winter-Hwen's Saga Like a great many Norse sagas, Winter-Hwen's seems to start in the middle of quite another saga, and to spend a lot of time putting the reader in some other picture, and introducing him to people he hasn't the least likelihood of ever meeting again. Some enjoy this sort of thing immensely. But if you're like the Infanta and find all this beginning a bore, then you'll just have to be patient. Winter-Hwen isn't going to change *his* ways—not after a thousand years. And, as Nossno says, the saga could be important.

Wolf-fang-raider See Strong-tooth.

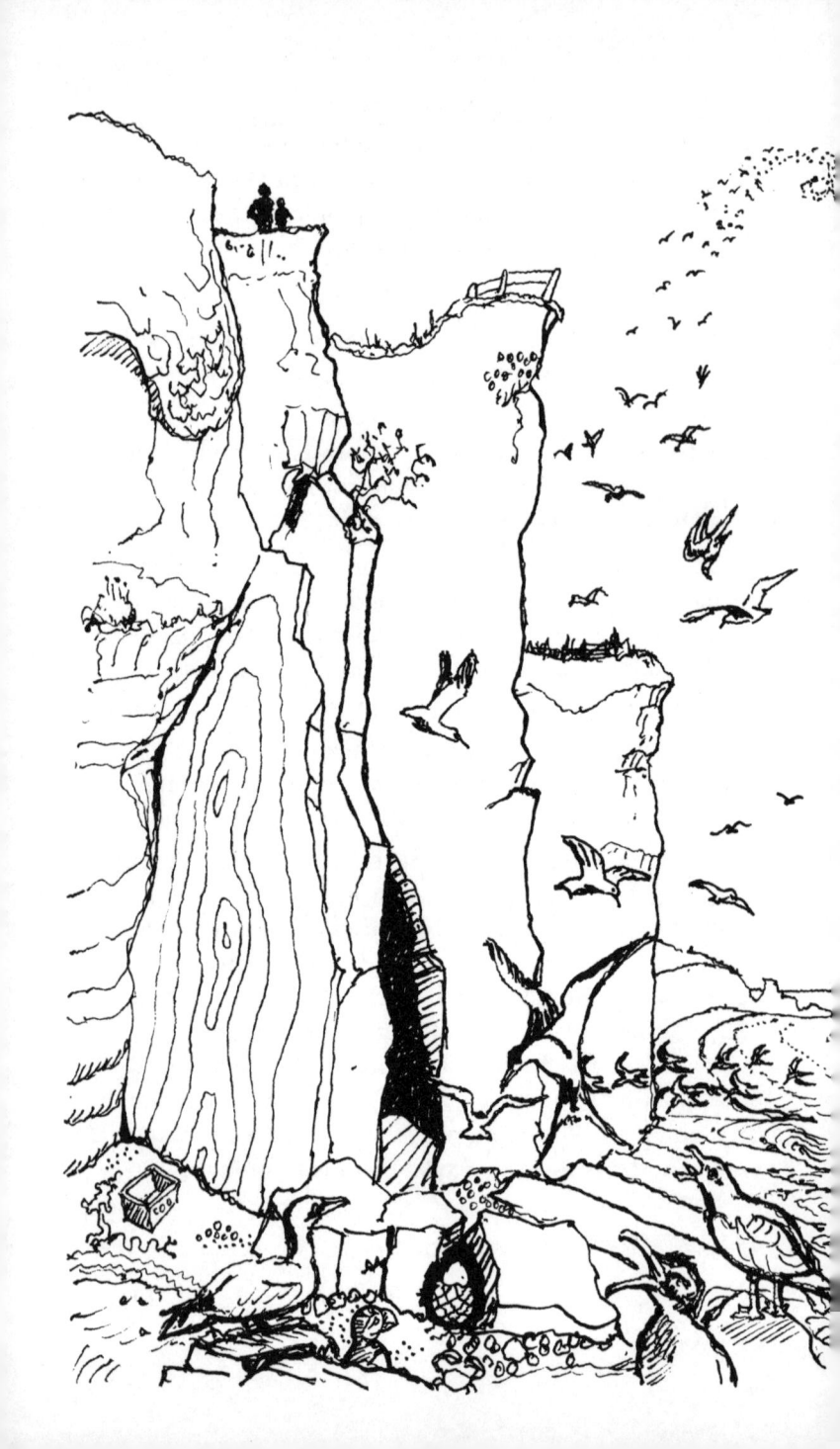

SPRING

"Phew, that was a near-squeak!" Buttonsson said. "Still, as it turned out, it should keep the Bartons quiet for a week or two—while they pull all the prickles out of each other."

And he laughed so hard he bent nearly double.

Buttonsson was coming back with Puttyboy through the woods. He was treading carefully to avoid the young bluebell plants just showing through the cover of winter leaves. And as he walked he was putting Puttyboy in the picture. He was telling him how Nossno reckoned the Bartons were stronger than ever this year and were hungry for blood.

"Nossno isn't afraid," Buttonsson explained, "but he is worried. He says the battle could go either way. The thing is that they've got time on their side, but *we've* got the riddle."

Buttonsson had been frowning, but now he laughed and it looked as if a patch of sky had opened in his eyes.

"Shall I tell you the riddle? Nossno made it up. Now all we have to do is find the answer. This is it:

I saw three ships come sailing by
One two three
Three two one
The first ship carrying the Moon-on-high
The second the Summer-sun

But the ship I see on Christmas Eve
Go sailing by
Over the sea
That ship is carrying the earth and sky
Holly and ivy and Christmas pie
And you and me.

You see, it's a good riddle. Christmas—you might say we have most of the year, plenty of time if it weren't that time's on their side. Bartons never run out of time. And they always have some to spare when it comes to killing. Three ships. Oh dear, I wish Rustass was more use with riddles. Still Nossno says that you, Puttyboy, could be the answer."

Buttonsson had stopped at the edge of the wood, and was now looking across the stretch of spring grass to the cottage. Outside the front door in the sunlight Rustass was sharpening the blades of the mower.

Buttonsson smiled affectionately.

"You see Puttyboy," he said, "Rustass is very strong and he's good with *things*, but with riddles he's just hopeless. He even thinks the Bartons is just *Mr* Barton. The trouble is he just can't *see* them. He doesn't *see* anything."

With Buttonsson stopped there at the edge of the wood, there is time to tell you of another thing that Rustass couldn't see. This was the tree that grew out of the roof of the cottage.

"I don't see it," Rustass had said when Buttonsson pointed it out. Rustass was a huge man, two and a half times as tall as Buttonsson. He'd been the friend of Button, Buttonsson's father. And ever since Button had died, killed it has been said by one of Barton's men,

Rustass had lived with Buttonsson and Buttonsson's mother Nancy, and had looked after them.

Their cottage had a straw-thatched roof, and walls called cob-walls made in a special way with mud and small stones and straw. It looked down the valley over the oakwoods and Mr Brewer's Wagwater Farm, where Mrs Brewer made her wonderful pasties, to the sea. The cottage was miles from anywhere except Wagwater Farm, and Barton Farm over the hill.

"You mean you really can't *see* it," Buttonsson had asked (or maybe he was simply explaining).

"Nope," said Rustass.

So Buttonsson had put him in the picture.

A jay had once dropped an acorn on the roof, he said, and it had stuck in the thatch. Before anyone noticed, it had become a small oak tree. Over the years it had grown. Its branches had grown upwards, much higher than the chimney, and its roots had grown down through the cob walls to the ground. In the summer its leaves gave shade to the cottage and kept it cool, and in the winter when the gales were blasting up the valley from the sea its roots held the cottage together. The roots also grew like twisted bars across the window of Buttonsson's bedroom. That meant that at night there was no chance of the Bartons climbing in through the window—they couldn't, not even if they'd not touched a tiddy-pasty all week.

"So now do you see?" Buttonsson had then asked.

"Nope," said Rustass.

So they had called Nancy, and she had run out of the cottage wiping flour from her hands into her apron.

"Oh yes, I can see it. I think it's a palm tree."

"It's an oak tree," said Buttonsson.

"Of course, an oak tree. He can't see it because he's so tall."

And she had reached up on tip-toe and given Rustass a kiss on the chin, and then had run back into the cottage to finish making the bread.

Anyway, Buttonsson was still stopped there under the tree on the edge of the wood. He was still talking to Puttyboy, putting *him* in the picture, and at the same time he was wondering how on earth Nossno could have known that Puttyboy would need meeting down on the beach. He was also thinking about the Bartons and wondering how they were to be done for before they succeeded in killing *everybody*. So with all this wondering going on, and before Buttonsson and the story get moving again, there's probably still just time to tell what Rustass had been doing that morning.

Soon after breakfast Rustass had come out of the cottage, sat down in front of the front door and begun to mend the mower. He used pieces of a bicycle he had found in a rubbish dump and some bits of wire and a lot of oil. The mower would be bound to work in the end because Rustass was good at mending things.

But what Rustass was *really* doing was worrying. He always worried when Buttonsson went off on his own, and that's what Buttonsson had done this morning. Of course Rustass knew that Buttonsson knew every path and sheeptrack and badger-run within four miles of the cottage. Buttonsson even knew the tracks which over the years the herons and the peregrines had worn in the sky. So he should have been quite safe. But there was another thing that Rustass knew. He knew that even a fox with all his cunning and his nose and ears and a memory that went back to William the Conqueror—even he might be caught in a wire snare if it had been laid by Farmer Barton.

So what Rustass was *actually* doing was listening.

Wind? Not a stir. Just a whisper from the sea—the tide must be far out, on the sand beyond the rocks. At the bottom of the valley the stream was chattering away. Over the wood and across two meadows Mr Brewer was taking his seven cows back to the field from milking. The cows were called Myrtle, Mo-ped, Mildred, Mainbrace, Marvel, Crewcut and Maxicrop. "Gin avore'm!" Mr Brewer was shouting to Scampi the farm dog, and one could tell from his voice that he was a kind man. Mr Brewer's kindness gave him a peculiar sort of strength. Even Farmer Barton would behave himself when he saw Mr Brewer. Farmer Barton had eyes red as a ferret's, orange hair, and a belly big as a hay-bale. But even so he had only to catch sight of Mr Brewer and he'd begin to smile in a sickening way and talk about the weather. This meant that Buttonsson on his walks was safe whenever he was on land belonging to Wagwater Farm. Anyway, "Gin avore'm!" Mr Brewer was shouting, and Scampi was barking with his mouth full which meant he had his teeth in the tail of one of the cows. Throughout all the countryside the woodpigeons had woken up to the spring. They were calling, but not all together. Each would wait politely for some other to finish, and then would take his turn: "Who whoo, oo-who who whoo?"

Nancy was spring-cleaning somewhere inside the cottage. Rustass could hear her sweeping and dusting and moving the furniture. These sounds were busy, but at the same time she was singing and that didn't sound busy at all. Her voice was slow and tuneful. *She* didn't seem to be anxious. This was her song:

> *The wind has moved West*
> *It shifted last night*
> *I woke this morning*
> *The garden was white*
> *The raven last evening*
> *Called winter home*
> *But this morning the blackbird*
> *And he was gone.*

Rustass lifted his head. For a time he appeared to forget about the mower, and during that time he seemed not so much to be listening as looking. Looking out from under his stack of black hair.

Down the valley in the V of the two hills was a piece of the sea, pale bluish-green, the colour of a song-thrush's egg. On the north side of the valley the gorse was in flower—like a spray of gold-dust on an ink-green quilt. White blossom was still out in the hedges and the brakes of blackthorn. Beside the cottage gate two puffed-up pink bullfinches were squabbling in the wild cherry-tree as they pulled out the first white petals.

But mostly Rustass was looking at the glistening grass. And mostly the small footsteps in the dew that led lightly away from the front door to a gap in the hedge.

So that was the way Buttonsson had gone—due west, into the oakwood.

At that moment there was a shout from across the valley. Rustass turned sharply and looked at Farmer Barton's big field up on the skyline. He didn't like what he saw, not one little bit.

Buttonsson was walking down the field, but not as

nimbly as usual. He was carrying something white in his arms. And across the field, hurrying to meet him, came Farmer Jack Barton and his fat dog, 'im's-Jack's. Rustass could see that Barton was carrying a bigger stick than usual; he could even see that the bristles were up on 'im's-Jack's's neck.

"I don't like it," growled Rustass. "Not one bit."

"Don't take on so," Nancy called out of the window. "He'll be all right."

And so it turned out because at that moment into the field immediately below Jack Barton's big field came Mr Brewer and his seven cows, Maxicrop, the black and white cow with the in-growing horn, first as usual.

"Good morning Mr Brewer," Rustass heard Buttonsson shout. Immediately the bristles went down on 'im's-Jack's's neck and he began to wag his tail.

"'Twill be proper zummer," Rustass heard Mr Barton shout to Mr Brewer, "if 'e don' rain drectly." And he waved his stick in the air in a friendly way, and smiled sickeningly.

Then Rustass saw Buttonsson nod to Mr Barton, and go on his way out of the field.

And that was that.

"Phew, a near-squeak," Rustass muttered, and went back to mending the mower.

Buttonsson had finished wondering.

"Come on, Puttyboy," he said. "I'll have to introduce you to Rustass again. He's bound to have forgotten."

He stepped out of the wood and started across the grass towards the cottage. Buttonsson's skin was weathered brown, the colour of honey. His eyes were wide and far apart and fine pale blue, as if he'd a patch of the sky in his head. His hair, as he walked into the sunlight, was a shock of yellow.

Rustass looked up from the mower.

"Hullo," he said, "that was a near-squeak with Farmer Barton."

"There, what did I tell you?" Buttonsson said to Puttyboy. "He thinks the Bartons is just Jack Barton. He just can't seem to see it."

Rustass frowned.

"What you got there?"

"This," said Buttonsson, "is Puttyboy."

Rustass leaned forward to examine Puttyboy more closely.

"Looks to me like a big ball of old tallow, half-wrapped in a bit of sack, and with a rope tassel sticking out of the top."

Buttonsson sighed.

"That's because you still can't see. Mum!"

Nancy came out of the front door. She had a green duster tied round her long fair hair.

"Mum, would you like to meet Puttyboy?"

"How do you do, Puttyboy. For a minute I thought you was just a big Easter egg. Still I hope you'll bide with us for a bite of dinner."

"Actually he *is* a bit of an Easter egg. In fact he could be *the* Easter egg. Anyway he's staying till Christmas. Nossno says he'll help with the Bartons. But Rustass thinks he's a ball of old tallow."

Nancy laughed. "That's only because he's so tall," she said as she went back into the house. "And he *has* mended the mower."

Rustass scratched around in his hair.

"Where did you find it. . .him, I mean, anyway?"

"Meet him, you mean. On the beach, exactly where Nossno said. But it's funny you don't know, because you were with me."

"Oh," said Rustass. He was still looking at Puttyboy, closely. Now he was scratching with only one finger, the back of his neck. "Well, I've forgotten," he said rather grouchily. "Perhaps you'll remind me."

"All right," said Buttonsson. "Let me put you in the picture."

Rustass appeared to stiffen. Then he looked up at Buttonsson.

Buttonsson was looking at Rustass. He was smiling and his blue eyes were full of pictures.

For a moment Rustass, as he looked into Buttonsson's eyes, had a strange creeping feeling on the back of his neck and up and down the nobbles on his great backbone. It could be bees, he thought vaguely—the bees that nested in the tree on the roof. But just as he was about to find out whether or not this were so, one picture in particular took his attention. He forgot about the bees.

The picture was that of a bird, a dipper, his white shirt-front spruce, perched on a stone in the middle of a stream.

Then Rustass got a shock.

The dipper began to rock backwards and forwards on his toes.

The picture was alive!

The stream was running past the rock with a deep gurgling sound. The dipper hopped in the air and when he landed again he had his back turned to Rustass. The level of the water was rising. It had almost reached the top of the rock.

"Sorry, dipper," said Buttonsson.

Rustass wondered how Buttonsson had managed to

get into his own picture. But there he was, in his boots, standing in the stream. And the picture was much bigger now. In fact Rustass could see right down the stream to where it flowed over the waterfall.

"Yik yik yik," the dipper said crossly as the water came to the top of his stone. He flew away.

Buttonsson laughed. And then Rustass saw him cross the stream and climb the bank on the far side.

Rustass hesitated a moment, and then he followed.

It was a high bank, overhanging at the top, but less steep below, and covered with violets, white and blue, and with primroses and brilliant celandine. The morning sunshine had found its way to them through the twigs and branches of the trees and they were now just beginning to open their petals. Unlike Buttonsson, Rustass had difficulty climbing the bank without trudging the flowers. When he did get to the top he looked around him. But Buttonsson was nowhere to be seen.

Rustass felt that the wood was very quiet and empty. But only for a short time. As he looked about him more closely, and as he listened more attentively, he changed his mind.

On the contrary the wood was very noisy and crowded. Everywhere he looked he saw the buds on the trees breaking into new green leaves. Nuthatches and woodpeckers and tree-creepers were running up and down the trunks. Mice, squirrels and blackbirds scampering or hopping over the ground. But no sign of Buttonsson.

"He's gone," Rustass said to himself, aloud.

"Top marks," he heard a sarcastic voice behind him say. "Top score. Top of the form. Top of the class. Topping. Tops. Observation of the century."

Rustass turned to see who this was. There was no one there. Or at least no one unless you count the enormous badger who a few yards away was busy scraping the last winter leaves from the porch of his deep-dug set.

Rustass felt foolish.

"How do you do?" he inquired, just in case it had been the badger who had talked.

"None the better for your asking," said a sharp cheeky voice behind him.

Rustass turned round quickly. There was no one there. Unless you count the small grey squirrel in the fork of a hazel tree.

"I'm getting out of here," Rustass muttered.

And as he started to climb the hill away from the stream the whole busy wood chattered with wisecracks and rude laughter.

There was a lane at the top of the wood (the lane that led to Mr Brewer's field), and beyond that a tall hedge full of ferns and rabbit-holes. And beyond that was the big field of the Bartons where the Bartons hunted hares and looked for trespassers, and shot with their shotguns and rifles at anything that moved. The big field stretched up over the hill, right away to the edge of the cliffs.

Rustass parted the young ferns and peered over the hedge to see whether there were any Bartons about.

"Don't worry about them," called Buttonsson. "They're still having their breakfast. Hurry up. Nossno says to look sharp or we'll be too late."

Buttonsson, with a grass in his mouth, was lying on his back in the field a few yards from the hedge. He was gazing up at the sky. He seemed to know without looking that Rustass was behind the hedge.

"Too late for what?" Rustass asked when he had

pushed his way through into the field.

"Puttyboy. Look, there's already something happening down under the cliffs."

Rustass looked.

The sky was full of large birds hurrying towards the sea. There were all sorts of seagulls, most of whom were screaming "Hurry-hurry-hurry-hurry." And there were ravens, rooks and jackdaws who were silent except for one or two who were croaking impatiently, "Come on. Come on. Come on." And there were a large number of black and white lapwings, flying quite out of control and screeching to each other "Be *quick!* Be *quick!*"

"See what I mean?" said Buttonsson jumping to his feet. "Come on."

And off he ran over the field. Rustass shrugged his shoulders and followed. He took one stride for every five of Buttonsson's. They didn't stop to look till they reached the edge of the cliff. From there they looked down.

Sometimes you get sunlight shining through a snowstorm. That's what the birds looked like as they fell and plummetted and plunged down the cliff-face in their hurry to get a good seat.

The tide was out, but the rocks weren't uncovered. North and south as far as they could see the rocks were hidden by birds all squabbling excitedly. And there right in the middle, four hundred feet down directly below Buttonsson and Rustass, was the centre of the excitement. Whatever it was, it was a white object.

"You see," said Buttonsson, "we're late. He's arrived already."

"That's him is it?"

"Yes, that'll be Puttyboy," said Buttonsson. "He's

come in from the sea. Everyone has been expecting him. Now we must go and fetch him. Close your eyes. And don't, whatever you do, open them."

Rustass closed his eyes. Immediately he felt a lot of wings about him, and wind, and heard the "ow-ow-ow" of the great black-backed gulls. And then he felt himself falling.

"*DON'T* open your eyes," he heard Buttonsson shout.

He felt his feet come down with a thud.

"All right, open your eyes," said Buttonsson.

Rustass opened his eyes. He was down on the rocks, looking up at the cliff towering above him. And Buttonsson was beside him. And there in front of him, stuck in a cleft between two rocks, was a white object. This, whatever else it was, was a large ball of white tallow with a piece of rope sticking out of the top, and half-covered at the bottom with an old bit of sack. Buttonsson introduced Rustass.

"This is Mister Rustass," he said, smiling at the white object in a welcoming way. "And this is Puttyboy."

With that, all the birds for miles up and down the coast squawked and flew into the air with excitement.

When they had settled again, Buttonsson said,

"Puttyboy's been in the sea for a year and a day. He knows all the answers. In fact Nossno says he could *be* the answer."

Rustass looked at the ball of old tallow with the tassel of rope sticking out of the top.

"*All* the answers?" he asked, doubtfully.

But just as he was asking the question he noticed something very odd. He was actually looking at the ball of old tallow when he saw this very odd thing. Deep inside the tallow, only just visible, were these two big eyes.

They were blue, and they were blinking slowly, and they appeared very watery, and were rolling around in a dreamy way. Sometimes they seemed to be looking at Rustass, and quite often they weren't.

"Yes," Buttonsson said very seriously, "*all* the answers. Go on, ask him a question."

Rustass tried to think of a question. At that moment there was a howl in the sky as a huge new jet plane flew past them low over the sea. All the birds flapped their wings and muttered angrily under their breath.

"What," Rustass asked, looking deep into the tallow at Puttyboy's eyes, "is the most expensive thing ever to fly?"

Puttyboy closed his eyes. They disappeared entirely.

"He's thinking up the answer," Buttonsson explained.

Then suddenly a small area in the front of the tallow began to swell, like a weak patch in a balloon. It came up in a lump. The lump grew into a big bubble. And suddenly the bubble blew up. It burst with a little plop like a bubble on the top of boiling porridge.

And out flew a small gold butterfly. For a moment it fluttered around Puttyboy, gleaming in the sunlight. Then it soared into the blue sky and flew glittering out over the ocean.

"See?" asked Buttonsson. And then, "Come on. Puttyboy must be starving. Besides we ought to get back sharp before the Bartons get onto our scent."

With that Buttonsson picked Puttyboy up from the rocks into his arms. Immediately all the birds for miles up and down the coast took off into the air and flew slowly and silently away. They shook their heads from side to side as if they had seen something so wonderful it had left them all quite speechless.

Buttonsson, carrying Puttyboy and running lightly

over the rocks, led Rustass to the foot of the cliff. And from there up a steep path that slanted across the cliff-face.

They had climbed the cliff and had just set out to cross the Barton's big field when,

"LOOK OUT!"

someone just behind them shouted. Rustass swung round. There was no one there. Unless you count the hare who was leaping away at great speed over the spring grass.

Rustass turned to Buttonsson.

But Buttonsson wasn't there either. And nor was Puttyboy. Rustass looked all about him. There was no sign of them.

Suddenly,

"BLARP—BLAR—BLerp. . ." went the hunting horn.

The Bartons must have finished their breakfast. There they all were, out in the next field up from their big field, hunting.

"BARK—BAR—berp. . ."

And so were their dogs. They were on to *somebody's* scent.

For a minute Rustass wondered what to do. Then, with his huge fists clenched, he walked away across the big field and climbed over the hedge, and across the lane, and went down through the wood to the bank of the stream just above the waterfall.

Rustass gave his head a violent shake.

He was back, standing outside the cottage, and looking down into Buttonsson's blue eyes. All the pictures had gone.

"Where did you and that—er. . .that Puttyboy get to?" Rustass asked.

"Oh, I thought you knew," Buttonsson said sarcastically, his eyes wider than ever. "I thought you said you'd been watching and had *seen* Puttyboy and me have that near-squeak with the Bartons."

Rustass sighed, as if he knew that what he was going to say would be all wrong.

"You mean *that* was it, when I saw you in Mr Barton's big field and Mr Barton. . ."

"There you are, Puttyboy," Buttonsson interrupted. "He's done it again. He thinks the Bartons is just *Mr* Barton. He can't seem to *see*."

"Now then, you two," Nancy called from indoors. "You stop your eternal chatter, and go and get washed for your dinner."

"We won't be a minute, Mum, honest." Buttonsson called back. "But I've *got* to finish putting Rustass in the picture."

"Oh no, not more!" Rustass protested. "Let's have our lunch first. I can't go off on any more sky-larking, not on an empty stomach."

But it was too late. Already his voice had begun to fade in his ears. Buttonsson was looking at him, and he was getting that creeping feeling again down the back of his neck.

Rustass was just thinking that this time it really might be bees, *the* bees, when he realized he was somewhere else. In fact he was walking up the path to the cottage from having been down to the sea with Buttonsson to meet Puttyboy. And thinking about bees he looked up at the bees' nest in the fork of the oak tree growing out of the roof of the cottage. Certainly it was very much alive. He saw four bees fly out, their wings making an angry whine, and then fly back in again.

"I think they're worried too," Rustass said to himself. And that reminded him how extremely worried he was about Buttonsson and Puttyboy. He stopped on the path, turned sharply, and looked across the valley to the Bartons' big field up on the skyline.

"Now let me see, hasn't all this somehow happened before?" Rustass was just saying to himself when. . .

"Blarp–BLAR–BLAR–Blerp–p–p–sshp. . ."

It was the sound from over the hill of a hunting horn blown by a man with too little wind and too much wet in his mouth. It was Mr Barton's hunting horn. The Bartons were onto somebody's scent. Or rather the Barton dogs were. There were six Bartons, father and five sons, and each had his own dog named after him. So the dogs' names were 'im's-Jack's, 'im's-Jan's, 'im's-Stan's, 'im's-Sam's, 'im's-Dan's, and 'im's-Len's. Each dog looked much like his master. And since each son looked like his father, Jack, all the dogs were fat with bloodshot eyes and orange bristles on their necks like autumn stubble. At the sound of the horn the dogs began to bark. The barking sounded something like the horn.

"BARK–BAR–BAR–Berp–p–p–ssshp. . ."

Too little wind and too much slaver.

Rustass was looking across the valley, watching the skyline. He had taken his hands from his pockets and had clenched his huge fists.

The bees' nest in the oak tree on the roof was sounding more angry still.

"BLARP–BLAR–Blerp. . ."

The Bartons were coming nearer.

"BARK–BAR–berp. . ."

And so were the dogs.

Over the skyline came a small figure, running. It was

Buttonsson in his boots, but he was not running as lightly as usual. He was carrying something white in his arms.

"Puttyboy," Rustass explained to himself. "So that's where they got to, is it?"

In the middle of the field Buttonsson stopped and looked back.

Over the skyline came the Bartons abreast. Each tugged by his dog on the end of a chain. Each carrying a long stick. The sun was quite hot, but still their breath, the breath of all twelve, men and dogs, came in a panting, steaming, heaving cloud. Altogether they weighed a hundred and seventy-two stone. So as they began to trundle and trip down the hill towards Buttonsson the ground shook both sides of the valley.

"Get moving," Rustass said aloud, his voice deep, like a wave breaking.

In their nest in the oak tree on the roof the bees were hopping mad.

But Buttonsson stayed where he was in the middle of the field. He seemed to be waiting for the Bartons to catch up. He was looking back at them over his shoulder.

As the hill became steeper, so the Bartons came faster. And faster.

When they were ten paces from Buttonsson they lifted their long sticks in the air and roared:

"Thick-wan'll larn you, bwoy!"

And with that Buttonsson began to run.

But he didn't run down the hill.

He turned round and ran up the hill straight at the Bartons.

Rustass growled and the bees' nest shook with fury.

THRASH! came the sound of the Bartons' sticks about Buttonsson's head.

But in fact these sticks were too long, and Buttonsson had been too quick for them. The points of the sticks stuck in the ground behind Buttonsson, and Buttonsson ran on up the hill.

Now the Bartons, tugged by their dogs, were going down so fast that their arms were jerked in their sockets. The right arms were jerked back by the sticks stuck in the ground, and the left arms were jerked forward by 'im's-Jack's, 'im's-Jan's, 'im's-Dan's, 'im's-Sam's, 'im's-Stan's, and 'im's-Len's.

"OUCH!" they bellowed. And as they rumbled past Buttonsson on down the hill they hadn't one hand between them to grab him by the scruff of the neck.

Buttonsson had slipped between the legs of Mr Barton, and run on to the top of the hill. He stopped there and turned and watched. He was still holding Puttyboy tight in his arms.

Rustass watched too. The bees in their nest had begun to unwind. Rustass chuckled.

On went the Bartons down the hill cursing and yelling and barking and trying without success to dig their heels into the soft spring turf.

There was another field below this field and the lower field belonged to Mr Brewer. In fact at this moment Mr Brewer had opened the gate in the bottom left-hand corner to let his seven cows in to grass.

Nothing could stop the Bartons now as they thundered downhill even faster than ever they had thundered before in their lives. Nothing except...

"OUCH OUCH YOW-OW-EEE-ARGH-OUCH."

WALLOP!!!

Nothing except the thick hedge of blackthorn, whitethorn, brambles and new sharp spring nettles that ran between the bottom of the Bartons' field and the top of Mr Brewer's.

The whole world was silent for a time, other than one towering skylark, and a funny noise coming from the oak tree on the roof of the cottage as if the bees were giggling.

Then two things happened together. Mr Brewer started to run across his field to see whether there was anything he could do to help the Bartons. And the Bartons tore themselves out of the hedge and started to yell at and blame one another, and to hit each other and their dogs with their long sticks. And 'im's-Jack's, 'im's-Jan's, 'im's-Dan's, 'im's-Sam's, 'im's-Stan's, and 'im's-Len's barked viciously and tore at the men's trousers and slashed at anything they could reach with their rotten teeth.

The noise was terrific. Until all at once the Bartons and the dogs looked up and saw Mr Brewer watching them over the hedge.

Immediately they began to behave themselves.

The men lifted their flat hats to Mr Brewer, and the dogs began to wag their tails. The men shook hands with one another, and brushed the prickles out of each other's clothes, and patted their dogs. The dogs grinned and licked one another, and rubbed themselves against the men's legs. Then the Bartons told Mr Brewer they hadn't hurt themselves very badly, and they wished him good day, and they said they reckoned it would be a good summer but it might rain directly. Mr Brewer said that if they weren't hurt that was a proper job, and that a drop of rain would be handy. Then he turned and walked away.

As soon as he turned the Bartons began to grumble

again, and the dogs to growl. Then the Bartons growled too and lifted their sticks and were about to hit out when they caught sight of Buttonsson on the skyline where he still stood looking down at them.

"VOOO-ALOOO, BWOYS!" screamed Jack Barton.

And with that they were off up the hill, puffing and humphing and cursing and groaning. The horn blared again, and the dogs whined and barked. But although the noise was terrific and the ground both sides of the valley shook, the Bartons didn't appear to advance up the hill at any great speed.

Buttonsson watched for a while as they gradually approached him. Then he turned and with a skip and a couple of light strides he was gone over the skyline.

"They'll not catch him now," Rustass said aloud to himself. "But that was a near-squeak."

A cloud of bees came out of the nest and calmly motored off down the valley to go to work on the gorse.

Rustass sat down, and continued to mend the mower.

"Any more for the sky-lark?" Buttonsson was saying.

Rustass gave his head a good shake.

"The only pity," Buttonsson continued, "is that Puttyboy didn't come in on a ship."

"Oh," said Rustass. He was still looking around him as if not altogether sure of himself. "And why's that a pity?"

"Because that would have been one clue to Nossno's riddle. Unless we can find three ships we don't stand a chance. Three by Christmas. Though perhaps it won't make any difference. The Bartons are growing stronger and stronger, and Nossno says they're almost bound to win. Summer, that's when they will attack again. We'll have to be ready."

"Three ships," Rustass was looking muddled. "But I thought you said Puttyboy would be the answer."

"*Could* be. But that's another riddle. Besides Nossno says that Puttyboy won't be ready till Christmas."

"I see," said Rustass.

Buttonsson smiled.

"That'll be the day," he said.

"Okay, okay," said Rustass. "But when do *I* get to meet this Nosmo or whatever-his-name-is?"

"Nossno. When you can *see*. But I don't expect that'll be much before Christmas either."

"Come along you two scallywags!" Nancy called from inside the cottage. "Dinner's ready. You come this instant or you'll have more than riddles to answer for."

"*Three* scallywags," Buttonsson laughed as he ran indoors. "Puttyboy's famished."

Rustass didn't follow at once. He stopped on the step for a minute to think. And while he thought he scratched his black hair on the underside of the thatch.

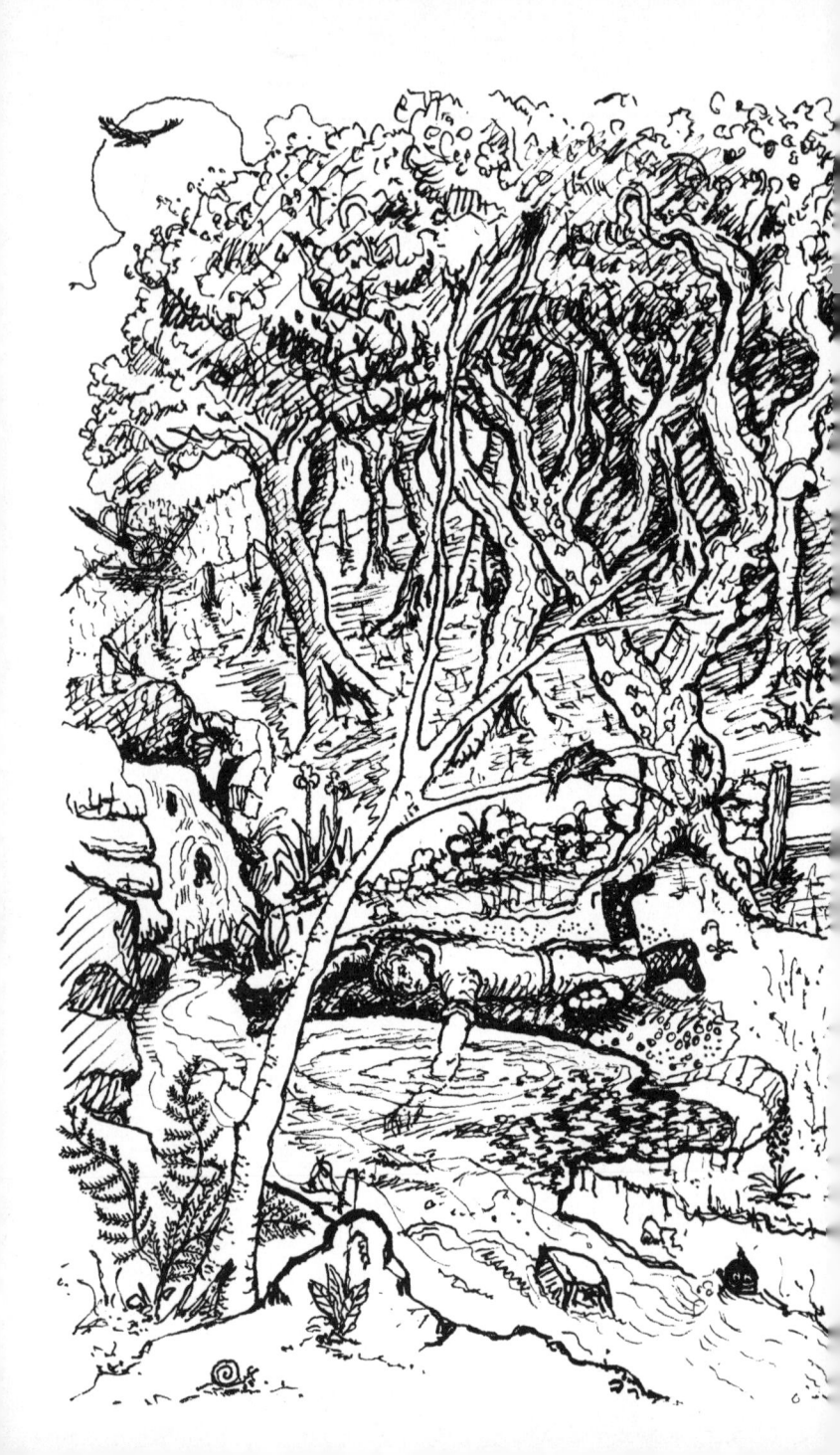

SUMMER

Puttyboy got an egg stuck in his eye.

"Is it a whole egg?" Rustass asked when he came down to breakfast. Buttonsson and Puttyboy had been up some time.

"Hard to say," Buttonsson said. He was over by the door putting on his boots.

Rustass went to the table to where Puttyboy was sitting, bent over and looked at him closely. To Rustass it simply looked as if half the shell of the boiled egg had been shoved into a large ball of old tallow.

"How did it happen?" Rustass asked.

"Not easy to tell," Buttonsson said vaguely. "It could be going in or it could be coming out."

Buttonsson seemed to have something else on his mind. He'd got his boots on and was standing and looking intently over to the big fireplace.

"Bees are busy," he said. "Hear them?"

Rustass listened.

"Nope," he said.

"You will," and the room seemed to lighten as Buttonsson smiled.

"Where are you off to?" Rustass asked.

"Off for a walk," Buttonsson said, "with Puttyboy."

"Watch out for Mr Barton."

"*The* Bartons. Yes, that's what Nossno says. Now it's summer they'll be looking for mischief. What about the ships? Half the year's gone and we haven't found *one*. We've only got till Christmas. Why don't you come and lend a hand?"

"I'm busy—inventing."

Buttonsson grinned.

"Oh good," he said. Rustass's last invention had been a kite that could loop the loop in a gale. "What's it this time?"

"That," said Rustass, "is *my* riddle. Why don't you ask Nosmo?"

"Nossno. But perhaps you'll come just the same. Remember?"

Rustass shook his head.

Buttonsson went and picked Puttyboy up from his chair and then turned for the front door. As he was going out he looked back over his shoulder and gave Rustass a peculiar look.

"We'll just have to *see* about that," he said.

That had been earlier.

It was now after midday. Rustass was sitting just outside the front door, working on his invention. He was taking to bits an old pram he'd found in a rubbish tip. But at the same time he was anxious about something— you could tell by the way he frowned. After a while he put the old pram to one side, and began to look about him. And as he looked he listened.

The entire world seemed flat on its back, basking; pleased with the sun, so long as it didn't intend to get even so little as a fraction of a degree hotter. At the end of the valley the sea was in a haze the colour of lilac. Just occasionally, Rustass would see a slow gleam on the surface, a twist in the swell, or a huge fish turning turtle. Nearer, in the valley, the fields were steaming. The air above them shimmered and twinkled, and was full of mirages of dew-ponds. Mr Brewer's fields were shorn and neat—*his* hay had been in bale and barn already a month.

Over the grass in front of the cottage several butterflies, blues and meadow-browns, were playing tag. They too seemed touched by the sun, they were so slow and aimless on their wings, bumping into each other and flopping about. Almost all the birds had packed it in. They were perched somewhere in the shade. Occasionally they would try to sing, but their voices seemed half smothered by the sweltering sunlight. Even Nancy's voice sounded distant. But her song was clear. She was upstairs, and although she was busy sewing she didn't sound hot. It was cool up there under the thatch.

This was her song:

> *The wind has gone South*
> *I don't recall when*
> *I slept one moment*
> *The garden turned green*
> *The blackbird last evening*
> *Sang it was spring*
> *But this morning the cuckoo*
> *And he was gone.*

Rustass stood up. But he was no longer moving his head this way and that. He was looking across the valley, through the shimmering air, at the big field of Farmer Barton. Mr Barton's hay hadn't been cut. It stood there sagging and overripe, with a shade of pink over the green where the grass and weed had run too far to seed. Rustass was thinking that next winter Jack Barton's cows would be chewing a bitter cud, and their milk would be brown and brackish.

But the next second Rustass had stepped out into the sunlight. From over the skyline of Mr Barton's big field came the ricketty sound of an old tractor being driven too fast. Could it have started the mowing? Not at that speed. Rustass with one huge hand shielded his eyes from the sun. Over the skyline came a small figure—Buttonsson. He was having trouble carrying Puttyboy through the tangled hay. Over the skyline a little to the right came the old tractor—Jack Barton driving with his head down, his shotgun cocked on his shoulder, powering through the hay to cut Buttonsson off.

"I don't like the look of it," growled Rustass. "Not so much as a little."

"Don't fret so," Nancy called out of the window. "He weren't born yesterday, not like Jack. He'll be all right."

And so it turned out because at that moment Mr Brewer, who had been bending down to mend some mischief to the water-trough (Maxicrop more than likely) his side of the hedge at the bottom of Farmer Barton's big field, stood up.

The tractor stopped on a sixpence and the engine jammed. The valley was silent.

"Good day, Mr Brewer," Rustass heard Buttonsson shout.

Mr Barton stood up in his tractor and raised his cap.

"Jed, 'tiz sticky," Rustass heard him call to Mr Brewer. "Would'n wonder 'twill thunder anon." He struggled to hide his shot-gun behind his back, and as he did so he gave a sickening smile.

Rustass saw Buttonsson nod to Mr Barton, and then make his way down to and over the hedge to join Mr

Brewer. Together they strolled off towards Wagwater Farm.

And that was that.

"Phew, a close shave!" Rustass muttered, and began to collect up the bits of the pram. He felt he'd done enough inventing for one morning.

Rustass had hidden his invention in the shed round the back of the cottage. Now he'd returned to the front door, and was standing in the shade of the thatch, waiting for Buttonsson to come home. The summer heat was settled over the cottage like a blanket. Silent, except for the occasional bumble-bee drowsing by, laden with pollen. And the sound of Nancy upstairs humming to herself.

In fact at that moment she had just taken a breath for some more humming when "OH NO!" she shouted.

Rustass heard her push back her chair, dash across the room and down the stairs.

"There's a go!" she called. "I've burned the dinner black's a cinder. O my, what'll ever we do!"

"We'll get by," Rustass said gently. "It's too hot for grub more than a mouthful."

"Who said aught about a mouthful," poor Nancy wailed. "Oh dear, when'll Buttonsson be back?"

"He'll not be long," Rustass said, and he turned to go into the cottage.

But he didn't go in. One foot on the step, and he stopped and listened.

There was the sound of light boots running on the grass track in the middle of the lane. A moment later Buttonsson came through the gate and up the path. He was carrying Puttyboy under his right arm. Under his left arm he carried a brown paper parcel. A yard or two short of Rustass he stopped.

"That," said Rustass, "was a close shave."

Buttonsson was still panting, but he managed:

"What's sweeter than Mr Barton's tooth?"

Rustass frowned and tugged at his ear.

"Honey?"

"So you *saw* it!"

"I saw Jack Barton try to cut you off with his tractor."

"So you *didn't* see it. Oh dear, Puttyboy, for a moment I thought he'd *seen*."

"Well," said Rustass, grouchily, "so what did you do then?"

"Hear that, Puttyboy? We introduce him to Royalty, and he doesn't even remember."

"Okay, okay, so what did *we* do?"

Buttonsson sighed, and then he gave Rustass another of those peculiar looks.

"It all began," he said, "it all began when. . . ." but suddenly his voice seemed to be wavering in the heat.

Rustass appeared confused. He looked up at the clear sky. He looked back at Buttonsson. Could Buttonsson really be saying that it had all begun when they struck the gold at the foot of the rainbow? Probably some old riddle.

"Takes rain to make a rainbow," Rustass said. But then he broke off. He noticed that Buttonsson's eyes were full of pictures. There was one in particular that took his attention.

This was the picture of a brilliant bird perched on a willow branch over the deep pool in the stream, just below the waterfall.

A kingfisher.

As Rustass looked the picture seemed to become alive. Ripples and bubbles moved across the surface of the pool. They reflected the sunlight onto the dry mud bank opposite, flashing like minnows caught in a shaft of light. But the kingfisher didn't move. It might have been stuffed. Nor did Buttonsson move. He was lying on his stomach on the near bank. He had an ear to the ground, as if listening. His forearm and hand were trailing in the water. Puttyboy lay on his back beside him.

Suddenly like a rainbow-missile the kingfisher dived at the pool. The surface exploded as if a stone had gone through the windscreen. But Buttonsson had been quicker, had grabbed with his hand and snatched out into the air something gleaming. Immediately he tossed the little silver trout to Puttyboy, who swallowed it with a plop.

"Sorry, kingfisher," Buttonsson said as the bird came out of the pool.

"Chip, chip!" the kingfisher called back indignantly, and away he went up the stream, a streak of gleaming orange and blue.

Buttonsson jumped to his feet and turned to Rustass.

"We're all behind," he said. "I'll go on. Do you mind bringing Puttyboy?"

Then stepping on two stones, he ran across the river. He scuttled up the bank on the far side, and was gone.

Rustass bent down to pick up Puttyboy. But then he started back in surprise. He could see beneath the surface of what looked to him like a ball of tallow Puttyboy's two big watery eyes blinking. And below that his blue moist waxy lips opening and closing like a fish's

43

mouth. But below that, down in Puttyboy's middle, there was a fish. It ogled out at Rustass with its brilliant white and black eyes.

It was a *gold* fish.

Rustass picked up Puttyboy and the fish and carried them gingerly under his jacket. He crossed the river, and with difficulty climbed the bank on the far side. Then he stood there in the green silent shadowy wood and looked about him.

"Now where's he gone?" Rustass said aloud.

"Pity he's got no ears," said a dry husky voice behind him. "Pity he makes such a noise. Pity he's got no nose. Pity he's got no eyes."

Rustass turned to see who was there. No one. Unless you count the sleek brown fox with the black tip to his brush who was padding away down a secret path.

Rustass felt nettled.

"Thanks for your help!" he growled after the fox—just in case it had been he who had talked.

"Yak-yak-yak-yak," came the crazy laughter behind him.

Rustass swung round. Nobody there. Unless you count the red-crested green woodpecker with bright bead eyes who was busy sticking his tongue as long as two worms into a crack in an oak tree.

"Come on Puttyboy," Rustass muttered, "let's get out of here."

And as he started to climb the hill away from the stream he had the feeling that the whole green silent wood was full of bright little eyes that were looking at him and smiling.

"Ah, there you are," Buttonsson called out as Rustass, carrying Puttyboy under his jacket, pushed his way through the hedge into the big field. "We were beginning to worry."

Buttonsson was sitting cross-legged in a large nest in the hay some twenty yards out into the big field. There was a girl with him.

"This," Buttonsson said as Rustass entered the haynest, "is the Infanta."

"How do you do, Infanta?" Rustass said solemnly. He looked awkward as he bowed because of Puttyboy under his jacket.

Very graciously the Infanta inclined her head.

"You can sit Puttyboy down here," Buttonsson said. "She knows about him already. Nossno's put her in the picture."

"No, you will give him to ourself," the Infanta pronounced in a haughty voice, holding out her arms. She took Puttyboy from Rustass into her lap and began to cuddle him. Clearly Puttyboy enjoyed this. Above where his mouth was, little bubbles came to the surface and popped, and then each one became a bubble of sound, like the chime of a silver bell, and floated away into the bright air, still ringing.

The Infanta smiled gravely.

"Good," she said, "we see Puttyboy has brought us a fish. I think Nossno is right, he might well be *the* answer when he's grown a bit."

Her hair was finer than silk, wavy, and black as the shiny side of a piece of coal. But her eyes were even blacker and even more brilliant—if diamonds were black, that would be the nearest thing to her eyes. Her skin was pale brown, with a glimmer of pink beneath, and her mouth was round and red. She was very beautiful.

She wore a white muslin dress, the hem of which hung well below her knees, and a patchwork apron of rich Spanish colours: olive green, silk blue and smouldering russet brown. On her feet she wore blue satin boots with shiny blue buttons up the side.

She looked up at Rustass, as if he were a line of low hills on quite the other side of her kingdom.

"If you please you may sit just here," she said.

Rustass looked a little confused, but he sat down.

"And now," said Buttonsson, "she's going to tell you her story."

The Infanta continued to look at Rustass, though now perhaps more as if he were merely an unknown sail on the sea's horizon.

"We are a throw-back," she began. "Three hundred years of barn and byre and bran, of breknis with muggettee Jack and zupper with Pudgy Dan and for all the difference it's made to ourself, tomorrow we shall be Queen of Aragon and Castille and Toledo. You may look at our eyes. Now listen. We'll tell you what these whisperings are.

"That is the crash of taffeta as the Infanta descends the great stairs. Those are the cries of the victims of the returning Conquistadors. That is the advice of the Grand Inquisitor, the poison being poured in your ears. While that is the chatter of my dwarf as he scampers around on all fours. Those sighs come up out of the dungeon from Christians who say the wrong prayers. That peppery sound? That's capsicum, a new delivery from the Azores. And that, Olé, is the midnight sound of a thousand Flamenco guitars.

"Now we'll tell you how it all happened.

"The Galleon set sail. . ."

"I beg your pardon?" Buttonsson interrupted. He'd sat bolt upright.

"I was saying," said the Infanta rather crossly,

"that The Galleon set sail. . ."

"Precisely," shouted Buttonsson, and rolled on his back with his legs in the air. "Hurrah! That's it. One anyway. One ship. But please carry on."

"Thankyou," said the Infanta icily. "Not just any ship, this was *The* Galleon, and it set sail from Cadiz bound for the Indies and a hoard of doubloons. The chief King of all Spain was on board. His name was Don Carlos and his eyes were fierce and proud and so black they made the night seem clear as midday. With him sailed his daughter, the beautiful dark-eyed Infanta. As soon as The Galleon left the harbour it was set on by a wind and blown north for three days and two hundred leagues.

"That wind never altered course. It was as if some witch or wizard or mage were talking to it. And the third evening The Galleon hit the rocks at the foot of Gallantry Beacon."

"That proves it," Buttonsson interrupted again, nodding his head wisely. "That's exactly where Puttyboy came ashore. So we do have one ship. Nossno will be over the moon. Even if," he added, "I'm not yet sure how the Moon-on-high fits into the picture."

The Infanta sniffed impatiently.

"Now where was we? It's not easy, even for us, being interrupted all the time. Oh yes, Gallantry Beacon. Well, waiting for the wreck in the half-light at the bottom of the cliff were six men. Actually it would have been only quarter light but for this spot of cold gleam that seemed to be just standing around and getting in everyone's way. None of us could think what that could be. . ."

"Could have been Winter-Hwen," Buttonsson commented. "He was probably trying to help."

"We *beg* your pardon," said the Infanta, as if someone had made a rude noise.

"Sorry, I forgot you hadn't met him. But you will. He could be important. Do please carry on."

"We are not to be interrupted again. Winter-Hwen indeed, whatever next. Well, as we were saying, there were six men. They had huge bellies, and orange eyes that glowed like lanterns. They wore flat hats and had long red whiskers on the backs of their necks like the bristles on a raddled pig. Halfway up the cliff behind them was another the same—only she was a woman, their sister, a horrid witch.

"She told them what to do. The Galleon broke up on the jagged rocks and the sailors swam for their lives through the white tumbling surf. But when they reached with their hands for a hold on the shore the fat men jumped on their fingers so that they fell back into the sea and were drowned.

"The King swam with the Infanta on his shoulders. When the witch saw this she was furious and told the sea and the fat men what to do. Just as the King stepped ashore, a freak wave leapt up and snatched the Infanta from him. The King turned to go back for her but the six fat men caught hold of him and tied him up with binder-twine and carried him up the cliff to the witch. On the way they passed close to the cold gleam, which actually seemed to be trying to get in the way.

"'If,' the King called to the gleam, 'you have any love in your heart, save my daughter. But don't touch her unless you're of royal blood.'

"With that, a wavering voice came out of the gleam.

"'I'm an earl's son,' it said, 'I'll do what I can, but without arms or legs it's not very easy.'"

"Yes, that's Winter-Hwen all right," said Buttonsson.

The Infanta closed her eyes for a second, and in this way managed to ignore him.

"The Infanta," she announced, "was never seen again. But not so the witch. She squinted and rolled her eyes at the King for a minute. Then what she said was this:

"'You can bring your maid back to the world if you like. But there is one catch.'

"'What's the catch?' asked the King, half mad with grief.

"The witch and her fat brothers looked at one another and they giggled a bit. Then the brothers said:

"'Us can't find any to marry thickee one.'

"They were all pointing at the witch.

"'All right,' said the King wearily.

"So the King and the witch were married.

"'Now,' said the King, 'where's the Infanta?'

"'Yer's a go!' said the witch. 'Didn' I tell'ee there was one catch?'

"'What's the catch?' the King asked.

"'You must have a child to get a child,' said the witch.

"'All right,' the King said, wearily.

"So they had a child.

"The witch, when she saw it, clapped her hands excitedly. It was tubby, with red eyes and red whiskers on the back of its neck.

"'A regular little Barton,' the witch cried out in delight.

"'But it's not the Infanta,' the King said sadly. 'Besides, it's a boy.'

"'Bwoys will be Bartons,' the witch decided. 'And remember, there's one catch.'

"'What be the catch?' the King asked.

" 'No one said aught about the first child.'

" 'All right,' the King said, wearily.

" 'Or the second,' the witch said, when the second baby was born tubby, with red eyes and red whiskers on the back of its neck.

" 'Or the third!'

" 'Or the fourth!'

" 'That seems to me like five catches,' the King said sadly when the fifth baby was born tubby, with red eyes and red whiskers on the back of its neck.

"The witch was beside herself with delight. She called the men and her sons together. And then she said to the King,

" 'Now I'll tell'ee the catch. Bwoys will be Bartons, but 'tiz the sixth child'll be a maid. He he he!'

"And while the Bartons laughed and hugged one another, the King simply died of grief and weariness.

"The witch was furious, but the men and the boys went on laughing. Which made her still more cross.

" 'Right,' she said, 'then you can have the catch.'

" 'What be the catch?' the men asked, looking nervous.

" 'Bwoys'll be Bartons,' she said. 'You'll see!'

"What happened was this.

"Thereafter whenever a Barton did succeed in finding a maid prepared to be his missis, their children were all boys. Even when the missis was one of twelve sisters, still it was boys.

"At first they said,

" 'Bayn't a lot to it. The sixth'll be a maid.'

"But then they saw the catch. There never was a sixth. Five bwoys, and that was their lot.

"It continued like this for three hundred years.

"All over the district, for miles around, people began

to use a new saying. 'Bwoys will be Bartons,' they would say to one another when they wanted to sound wise. But no one seemed to know quite what it meant.

"Then after three hundred years came mump-head Jack. He took even longer than most other Bartons to find himself a missis. In fact he had all but given up looking, when this maid came and found him. Which was odd for a start. At first everything went as usual. Jan. Dan. Sam. Stan. Len. Five bwoys, all tubby with red eyes and red whiskers on the back of their necks.

"'And that's your lot,' Jack said to the missis.

"But the missis smiled to herself.

"'Us'll zee about that,' she muttered. And she hurried into the kitchen and began to make a pudding.

"Next thing Jack knew there was a shout from upstairs.

"'Jack, do-ee come and zee the zixth then you.'

"Jack trundled up the stairs with Jan, Dan, Sam, Stan, and Len in a line behind, all blubbering in case it was too good to be true, and just another bwoy after all.

"They lined up round the cot.

"Ten minutes later Jack said:

"'Reckon 'tiz the Invanter.'

"He and the bwoys took off their flat hats and stood there beside themselves, giggling politely.

"The babe had fine black hair and her eyes. . .why, if diamonds were black that would be the nearest thing to her eyes. Her mouth was round and red, and she was very beautiful.

"But now we're a baby no longer. They keep us, the Infanta and, for all we know, the Queen of Aragon and Castille and Toledo, in a strong room above the attic and under the thatch and three layers of slates. Every evening for hours we hear Jack and the bwoys squabbling and scrapping, bickering and bludgeoning and biffing one another as to whose turn it is to bring us our supper. Our supper is always late. And it's always the same: tiddies and whey.

"That's our story. And now, if you please, listen."

        put put put   BANG! BRmmm

rimmm   Clang CRASH!

BruMM B   whurrawurra

    rrrh   Bang burrrerr Brmm

      SPLUT...!   bRRRmmmmmmmm...

Clanger burrmurrah rrmm...

Six lines of crotchetty noise, all at once and out of time.

"Oh dear," the Infanta said, "that will be them now. Coming this way. If they find us we'll not see the sky ever again."

Buttonsson leapt to his feet and grabbed Puttyboy.

"Leave this to me and Puttyboy," he said.

"Puttyboy and me," the Infanta corrected sternly. "But he is brave," she added as Buttonsson, running lightly, disappeared over the skyline of the big field.

BaaaarrrRRRUUMMM!!!!!!!

Over the skyline the tractors had caught sight of Buttonsson and were after him.

"Very brave," and for the first time the Infanta's voice wasn't haughty; it was soft and a little bit tender. "If they've found out that us is meeting him like this, oh dear. That would be why they so want to catch him. We dread to think what they'd do if they did. But we wouldn't be able to eat for a month—not stew. Just in case. Ugh!"

She shuddered. But then pulled herself together and looked at Rustass again for a minute, distantly, as if possibly he was the messenger on the horizon, but more likely just a small cloud of dust.

"Kindly hand us the fish."

Rustass looked. Where Puttyboy had lain in the hay was the goldfish in a little glass bowl. He picked it up and gave it to her.

"You may kiss our hand if you wish," she said.

Rustass stood and bent down and kissed her hand.

"Your audience is over," she said.

Rustass looked confused for a moment. Then he turned and walked away. He climbed over the hedge, and crossed the lane, and then went down through the wood to the bank of the stream just above the waterfall.

Rustass gave his head a good shake.

There he was, outside the cottage, looking down at Buttonsson. Buttonsson's eyes were clear, all the pictures had gone. And he kept shifting his hold on the brown paper parcel, as if it had begun to get hot.

"That girlfriend of yours," Rustass said. "Phew!" And he wiped his forehead with the back of his wrist.

"Oh her. . ." Buttonsson said trying to sound vague, but blushing a little. "Still she did come up with a ship."

"Don't see how *her* ship could help anybody."

"No more you do. But then I don't suppose *you* could see how three ships would help—supposing we could find the other two. The Bartons are getting stronger by the way. As the year gets older, so they grow stronger—that's always the way it is. Come the autumn we'd better look nimble—after what happened this morning. Twist the tail of a Barton and his eyes go pink, that's the sign he's thirsty for blood. Thirstier he is, the stronger he be."

"That reminds me," said Rustass, "where did you get to, you and that. . .er, that Puttyboy?"

"I thought you said you *saw* Jack Barton given a close shave."

"Jack Barton?" Rustass said in some confusion. "No, I don't think I said Jack Barton."

"Oh," said Buttonsson and shrugged his shoulders. "I must have misheard." But at the same time he seemed to be taking a close look at Rustass—a close and peculiar look.

Rustass saw the sky turn over once. He felt queer for a second and then he found he was coming up the path to the cottage. He'd just got back from his audience with the Infanta. He was worrying about what had happened to Buttonsson and Puttyboy when he noticed the disturbance up in the oak tree that grew out of the thatch. News was coming in. The entire bees' nest was muttering. A number of bees came out and stood around in the air in a busy way making a menacing buzz. Then he heard something else. He turned sharply and looked back across the valley to the skyline of the Bartons' big field.

r. .upPP   BANG

bRrr!mM— Ber   brm!   Splutter   Berrummmm

         rUm.!   RRawuHrrah . . .!   MMM!

BerRrrM.   Bu   whirrumm. .   Parp

     BANG   BANG

  urp — clapper clapper clapper. . . .   brmmmm. . .

Six lines of sound from over the hill.

Six tractors in fact.

The six old crotchetty tractors that belonged, one to Jack Barton and one to each of his five sons. If the Bartons went mowing they went together, each driving his tractor. They steered with their boots and kept their hands free to handle their shot-guns. So that they could shoot at anything in the grass that happened to move. Their dogs would go with them—that's 'im's-Jack's, 'im's-Jan's, 'im's-Dan's, 'im's-Sam's, 'im's-Stan's, and 'im's-Len's—each one gollopping along beside a tractor, too puffed to bark.

Rustass had taken his hands out of his pockets, and had clenched his huge fists. But nothing was moving on the skyline of the big field—except the air, which even from across the valley he could see shifting and rising like fumes from a petrol tank.

The oak tree on the roof sounded as if a breeze were passing through—but this was simply the wind-up in the bees' nest.

      put put put   Ban. Brmm

 rimmm   Clang clash . . .!

bRum b   whurrerrerr

    rrrer   BANG burrrrer brrum

     splut . . . !   bRRmmmmmmm. . .

futter-put futter-clap clatter-pat. . . whurrah wurrah

                                        Bum.

The tractors, all six of them, were coming nearer.

Over the skyline of the big field came a small figure, running.

It was Buttonsson in his boots. He was carrying Puttyboy. He had to skip, keeping his knees high, to be clear of the Bartons' hay that tried to snatch at his ankles. He was some way down the hill towards the bottom of the field when he stopped and looked back.

Over the skyline on their tractors came the Bartons abreast.

On one side of each tractor gollopped a fat dog.

On the other side slithered the sharp clippers.

As the tractors began to trundle down towards Buttonsson, the ground shook both sides of the valley.

"On your way," Rustass said aloud, his voice urgent.

In the air above him the bees had formed up in the shape of a cigar. The cigar was fuming.

"VOO-ALOOO, BWOYS," screamed Jack above the racket of the tractors.

Buttonsson turned and began to run with Puttyboy down the hill.

Five paces.

Then his boot got caught in a snare of goose-grass. Over he pitched head first into the hay.

BANG-BANG

The Bartons let off both barrels together. Then they did something regrettable. They were all so eager to be first to see whether they had winged Buttonsson that they threw up their guns, and grabbed their hayforks, and leapt down from their sluggish tractors.

Len landed on 'im's-Len's and was badly savaged.

Stan jumped the wrong side, fell on his bottom and had the seat mown out of his breeches.

Sam and Dan leapt well clear, but pitched in a heap together, prodding each other with their forks. 'Im's-Sam's and 'im's-Dan's thought they were fighting. So they bared their stumpy teeth and attacked. The whole heap of them lost its temper.

Jan leapt hardest, but missed his footing. Somehow his belt got hitched over the tow-bar. He was towed away by his tractor.

But Jack knew better. He flopped onto his great belly and let himself roll till he stopped. Then he heaved himself to his feet, sniffed the air, and started after Buttonsson.

Buttonsson was nowhere to be seen. He and Puttyboy were still caught up in the hay.

Rustass ground his teeth. The bees shot off like an arrow, leaving behind them the whine of a taut bowstring.

But meantime what of the tractors?

The tractors were busy getting on with the job of mowing the big field. Most of them worked in circles, big circles or small circles, some left about, some right about. They choked and spluttered, but they stuck to the job. Barton's sons and their dogs had to look lively not to be cut to rashers. They cursed and swore and yelped and biffed at each other as they fought to keep clear of the cutters.

But two of the tractors had other ideas.

Jan's tractor just kept going straight. Which meant that Jan, hitched by his belt to the tow-bar, kept going straight as well. Straight on down the hill, straight through the hedge, straight down through the great gorse patch, straight over the bank and with a splash straight into the stream. So Jan's tractor was knocked out, and so, we can take it, was Jan.

Jack's tractor turned slant across the field. It crashed through a gate in the hedge and was last seen cutting a clean swathe across Mr Brewer's field.

Sam's and Dan's tractors met head on. For a time they grunted and strained and roared as they tried to push each other out of the way. But then suddenly they broke down completely. They just stood there together in the middle of the field, silent and smoking blackly.

Len's tractor and Stan's tractor also collided. But not head-on. They somehow got locked together, and side by side they started up the hill straight at the heap of Sam and Dan and their dogs. And now in fact Len too, and 'im's-Len's—after their own scrap they had felt here was too good a temper for them to miss.

Working together, Len's and Stan's tractors showed a good turn of speed up the hill. There seemed every chance they would mow the whole yowling and yelping heap to slivers. But at the last moment Sam, Dan and Len looked up. Immediately they took their teeth out of each other's legs, dropped their hay-forks and ran. Len's and Stan's tractors followed on their heels, straight up the hill and over the skyline.

Now all the tractors had gone and suddenly the valley was quiet. Rustass could hear in the distance a little whimpering noise. It was Stan up there in the big field on his hands and knees searching in the hay for the seat of his breeches.

Meanwhile what of Jack?

Jack was stalking through the hay with his fork held ready above his head like a harpoon. But there was no sign of Buttonsson.

Wait.

Yes, there he was.

"Dawntee move bwoy," yelled Jack, "else I'll stick thee like a peg on a skewer then you."

Buttonsson didn't move. He was on his knees in

the hay not two yards from the front of Barton's belly.

"As tiz," Barton bawled, "I reckon I'll spit thee just the same.—Yer's a pin for thee, maggot."

And he raised his hayfork in his pudgy fist to strike at Buttonsson.

Rustass, as he looked across the valley at what was going on in the big field, had begun to let out a great roaring growl.

But he stopped.

For some reason Jack Barton had dropped his hayfork. The reason could have been that he had begun to grow a beard.

Yes, it was odd, but quite clearly he was growing a beard.

Rustass saw him put his hands to his chin. The beard grew over his hands. Barton began to hop around in the hay.

"OWWWWOOOUCH!" he yelled, and Rustass, right across the valley, could hear the angry buzzing of his beard.

Buttonsson was now standing up. He was holding Puttyboy cradled against his tummy, and he was trying not to laugh.

Buttonsson said something. It was not easy to understand what he said, but as soon as he had said it, Mr Barton's beard flew away. It took off from his chin, hovered once round his head and then simply flew away.

Immediately Jack grabbed up his hayfork again. But Buttonsson had begun to run. Jack Barton went after him. Round in a circle ran Buttonsson through the hay. Once. Twice. Barton trundled behind.

"I'll 'av 'ee," he panted, and thrashed the air with his hayfork.

Buttonsson stopped in his tracks.

"Ha-HA," Barton yelled, and lifted his hayfork for the final prod. But before the prod could get under way, came the sound of a tractor.

Barton looked round. He dropped the hayfork as if it had turned into a longcripple. He was brushing the hayseeds out of his hair and sprucing himself up. In fact he began to behave himself.

And into the field, through the shattered gate, came Mr Brewer. He was returning Barton's run-away tractor.

"Caught 'im trying to climb a tree," Mr Brewer said when he'd pulled up the tractor beside Jack Barton.

"Well I'll be blessed," said Jack, raising and lowering his cap as fast as he could, and smiling and winking with alternate red eyes.

Mr Brewer looked round the big field, and Barton said he and his bwoys had been trying a new method of mowing they'd read of in Varmer's Weekly, and that it might rain directly and that a tidy drop wouldn't go amiss once the hay was in.

"I think I'll go along with Mr Brewer, if you don't mind," Buttonsson said.

"That's all right, me buddiful," said Jack, and his sickening smile was lost somewhere in his chin which already in a number of places had begun to swell like a protruding inner tyre.

"Good riddle," Rustass laughed. "What's sweeter than Jack's tooth is the honey in his beard. So that was the closest shave."

He looked around and was surprised to find that Buttonsson wasn't there. But then he heard him inside talking to Nancy. Rustass turned and looked in through the front door.

"For me?" Nancy was saying.

She wiped her hands in her apron before taking from Buttonsson the brown paper parcel.

"A present? There's precious little for dinner, so I hope 'tisn't Christmas."

"Better not be," said Buttonsson. "With only one ship we'd all be sunk. Except the Bartons. They'd be cooking *our* goose!"

"What can ever it be?" said Nancy. She held the parcel to her cheek. "Why, 'tis hot's a hay-pook."

"Yes, it's the answer to the hottest riddle."

Nancy set the parcel on the table and unwrapped it. Then she stood back and put her hands over her mouth.

"My, bless us all!" she whispered through her fingers. "It's a gurt pasty."

Buttonsson grinned.

"Mrs Brewer made it for Puttyboy, but he says we're all welcome to a slice. A *gurt* big slice!"

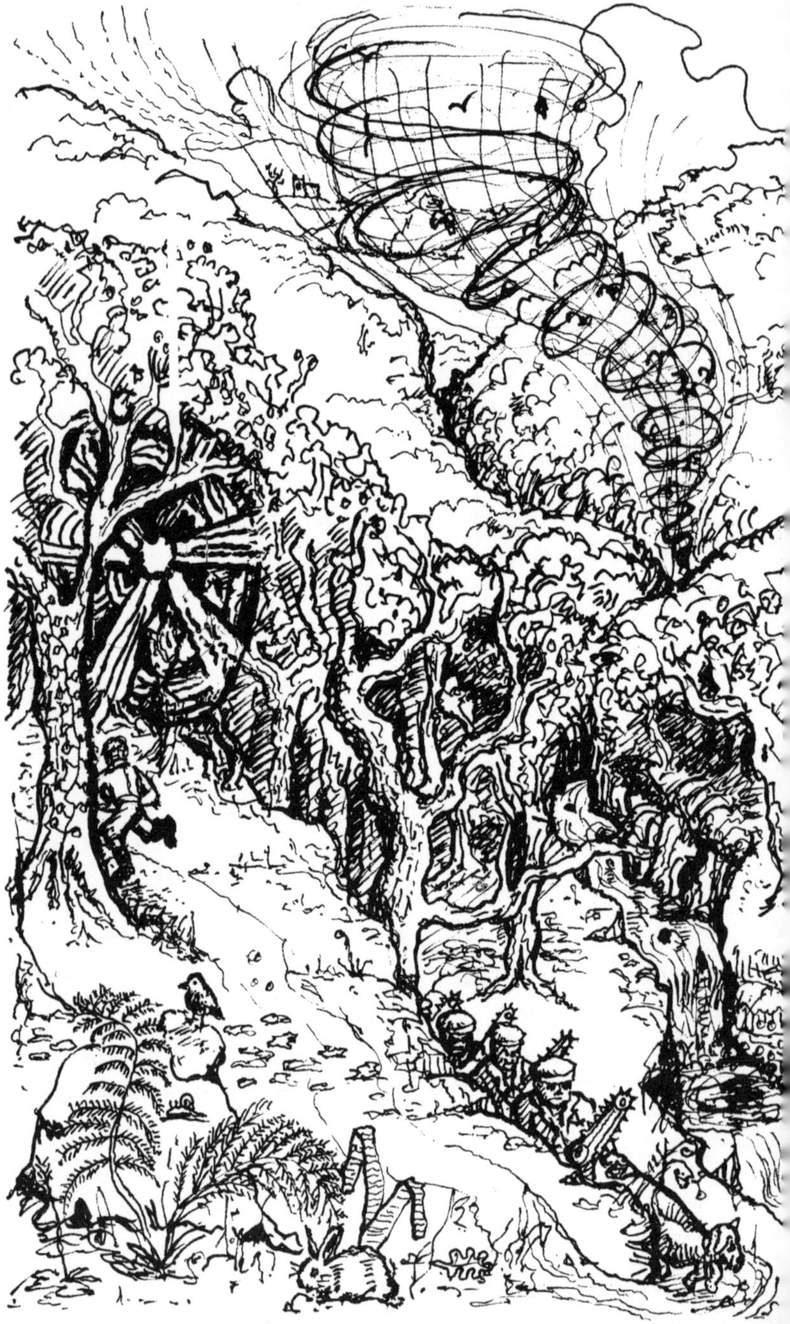

AUTUMN

Rustass was just back from the rubbish dump.

Earlier that afternoon he'd been working on his new invention. He'd fitted the pram-wheels—no hitch there. Then he'd tried to start the engine—nothing, not a spark of life. So off he'd had to go to the dump to fetch the spare part. That hadn't been easy, but finally he'd found the bit that would do the job—a coil in an old vacuum cleaner.

But now, back at the cottage, he didn't for some reason appear eager to return to work. Perhaps because it was late in the afternoon, almost twilight. Anyway there he was outside the front door, with his collar up, his shoulders hunched, his hands in his pockets, standing in the wind.

"What. . ." he began. But the wind whipped the word from his lips. He grimaced as if he had toothache.

"When does a. . ." he tried, but the wind blew the words into the thatch.

Rustass shook his head angrily. Just a second or two earlier he'd had this idea for a riddle. The idea was clear, but no matter how he tried he couldn't think how to dress it in words. This was the idea:

The warm September gale was piling in off the sea. It was trumpeting up the valley and heaving through the woods and scything and whistling through the hedges and the grass. It was bundling the birds out of the sky and replacing them with leaves, bits of bracken and straw, and big wadges of spume that it had ladled out of the rock-pools down on the beach. But even so, and above all this racket, Rustass could hear, somewhere down in the valley and coming closer, a lull in the gale. Very odd. The gale was roaring, but there behind it, he could hear quite clearly—nothing. That, for certain, was a riddle to fox Buttonsson, if only he could discover the way to ask it.

BANG

Or rather not bang at all. The lull had arrived, and the wind was scampering away inland, its noise seeming very puny beside the sudden

SILENCE.

"When is a wind not a wind?" Rustass tried. But the silence didn't seem impressed.

Rustass shook his head sadly. Then he stopped. All of a sudden he was listening. He looked up at the roof. It sounded to him as if someone was up there, perhaps just over the ridge of the thatch, singing.

"Must be another riddle," Rustass said suspiciously.

The tune was happy enough, and in fact the voice sounded like Nancy's.

This was the song:

> *The wind has moved East*
> *The year's growing old*
> *I caught her whisper*
> *The garden turned gold*
> *The cuckoo last evening*
> *Called summer in*
> *But this morning the robin*
> *And he was gone.*

Rustass laughed.

"I've got it," he murmured, "she's laying the fire!"

He was right. And so the answer to the riddle was that the song had floated up the chimney and was being broadcast outside so that it seemed part of, or at least something to do with, the lull in the gale.

Rustass looked away again, down the valley. The sea was choppy as a field of kale, and precisely as green. Except where the great Atlantic waves uncovered their white spines and ran broadside at the land. As Rustass watched, a part of the ocean darkened—a new chapter of the gale was coming in. And as if to be sure no one would doubt it, a cold fitful breeze, full of rumours, gusted through the lull.

Rustass at that moment understood what he had really been thinking all along. How it was autumn. And how with Jack Barton about it would be best if Buttonsson were home before dark.

There'd been trouble at dinner.

When Nancy had brought the soup to the table, she'd exploded and nearly dropped the tray.

"I'm sick to death of that Puttyboy," she said. "Look, there are bits of him all over the table. 'Bout time he found somewhere else to live."

Rustass looked at Buttonsson. Buttonsson looked at Nancy, and he swallowed—something big and lumpy.

"But," he said in a small voice, "he'll be gone by Christmas, Bartons or no Bartons."

"I think it's the way he behaves," Rustass suggested, though it wasn't quite clear to whom he was speaking.

"Then he should mind his manners," said Nancy, and in spite of herself she smiled.

Buttonsson was quiet for a time. But when it came

to the apple-pie, "Good-O," he said, and bolted it.

"What's the hurry?" Rustass asked.

"Hurry? What's the answer to the commonest riddle?"

Rustass scratched the back of his neck with one finger.

"I give up," he said.

Buttonsson grinned.

"That's right," he said. "But do ask me another one later. The hurry is to be ready in time for Christmas. Nossno thinks we're getting dreadfully behind. He thinks we may all have had it already."

Rustass frowned.

"But it's ages since we saw hair or hide of Farmer Barton."

"*The* Bartons. Yes, that's the trouble. Can't you see what they've been up to?"

Rustass didn't answer.

"Anyway," Buttonsson continued, "the immediate hurry is that it's now the autumn, and Puttyboy has an appointment."

"Who with?" asked Rustass.

Buttonsson looked at Rustass, almost a peculiar look.

"You'll see," he said.

He got down from the table and collected Puttyboy from his chair.

"Perhaps he's going to see the oculist," Rustass suggested. "Perhaps he'll get the egg out of Puttyboy's eye."

"If Puttyboy *had* an egg in his eye. Hadn't you noticed? He's got a *glass* eye now."

Rustass looked down at the glass eye and nodded uncertainly. To him it looked more like a jam-jar—an old jam-jar stuck into a ball of old tallow.

"Well, keep one eye open for Mr Barton," Rustass said grimly.

"And one eye open for blackberries," said Nancy.

And then Buttonsson had run to the front door.

"Don't worry," he had called back as he went out. "We'll be home for tea."

So now it was twilight, and Rustass, outside the front door, was attending to the lull in the gale. Not that there was much of it left. In fact Rustass could see down the valley the first breaker of wind beginning to churn the gorse on the hillside beneath Farmer Barton's big field. In a moment or two it would be into Mrs Brewer's chimney, gusting the smoke back through the door of her oven. And then it would be across the lane and into the oakwoods.

As Rustass watched the gale approach, he suddenly clenched his great fists. Was it something he heard? The wind perhaps, because the renewed sound of that was already quite clear. Or the silence? Because that too was still clear, very clear.

No wait! What was this?

BrrrrrrrrUMMMMMMM rmmmm rmmmm RMMMMMMMMMMMMM

The noise was fearsome. Then a moment later, just before the wind hit the cottage, came the crack and crash of a tree falling in the wood.

Rustass narrowed his eyes.

"Jack Barton," he growled, and the wind snatched the word off his lips and carried it echoing away inland like a warning.

So Mr Barton was out with his chain-saw. He didn't care for trees.

The day appeared to darken with the gale. Rustass

stared down the valley. Everything seemed to be swaying and ducking away from the wind, and now no sound apart from its roar could make itself heard. Was the chain-saw still busy? Rustass turned his head this way and that, but his hearing could find no line through the wind. In fact the wind was behaving like one giant chain-saw; its teeth were into the valley.

So Rustass relied on his eyes.

Two seagulls were blown by, flying backwards. Then a number of crows, all out of control, shouting orders at one another which no-one could hear. Now when a gust hit the wood below the cottage leaves would fly, like orange sparks from under a hammer.

But look! Over there. Was that something moving in the Bartons' big field?

But as Rustass looked, the wind slashed at his eyes and filled them with tears. Rustass wiped them clear with the sleeve on the back of his wrist. He shielded his eyes with both cupped hands and looked again.

There along the bottom of the big field, heading in the direction of the sea, trotted Buttonsson. He was holding Puttyboy in his arms. They must have broken through the hedge from the lane at the top of the wood. They ran a hundred yards and then stopped and looked back.

Along the hedge behind them, head down into the wind, waddled this great hulk of a figure. Jack Barton. As he waddled he was hoiking at the coil start of the chain-saw, eager to get the blades spinning again, keen to do someone an injury. Then twenty yards short of Buttonsson he stopped in his tracks.

Buttonsson had appeared simply to ghost through the hedge. And now he was making his way, almost gliding it appeared, down through the great gorse patch.

Barton on tiptoe watched him over the hedge. How could Buttonsson do it? Perhaps there was a fox-track or a badger-run. Buttonsson reached the bottom of the hill. For a moment he disappeared down the bank of the stream. Then he came out on the other side. He was safe—this field belonged to Mr Brewer.

Jack Barton turned, and was bundled up the field by the wind, and disappeared into the gloom.

The front door opened behind Rustass.

"Tea'll be ready directly," said Nancy. "Where's Buttonsson?"

"He'll be home," Rustass said, "in time for tea."

"What's that old thing?" Nancy asked.

Rustass looked down to where she was pointing.

"That's my invention."

Nancy clicked her tongue and smiled affectionately.

"Boys will be boys," she said as she closed the front door.

Rustass bent and picked up the bits of his invention.

"No, boys will be Bartons," he said aloud to himself. And as he walked round to the shed at the back of the house, he wondered where he had heard *that* before.

Just as he got back to the front door the wind dropped again and he heard the sound of light wellingtons out in the lane. He watched Buttonsson come through the gate and half-way up the path. There Buttonsson stopped, with his head on one side, and grinned up at Rustass.

"Well?" he asked.

"What's quieter than singing and louder than the wind?" Rustass asked.

"I know that one. A lull in the storm. But I've got one for you. When does the chimney stop singing?"

"The answer to that," Rustass said grouchily, "is, 'When Nancy has finished laying the fire.' I should know. It's my riddle."

"Oh, sorry," said Buttonsson, and he laughed till he nearly fell over.

"Well," Rustass said stiffly when the laughter had finished, "and how did Puttyboy get on with his appointment?"

"You mean you can't remember? You were there too, you know."

In the gathering dusk Buttonsson's blue eyes, as they smiled up at Rustass, looked like the last shreds of daylight in a winter sky. Something cold ran down the massive nobbles on Rustass's spine—it could have been a drip from the thatch, or a feeler of the wind. Buttonsson's eyes darkened, as if a cloud had come. But then Rustass saw that the cloud was moving. And then he saw that the movement was the ripples stirred by the wind on the surface of the pool beneath the waterfall.

"We've been waiting for you, you know," Buttonsson said a little severely.

Rustass looked up.

Buttonsson and the Infanta were standing side by side, looking down at him from the top of the high bank on the far side of the stream. The Infanta's gaze was vague and disdainful, as if the figure across the wide Tagus River might or might not be the herald of the untrustworthy Franks. The wind was blowing the loose bits of her black hair. She looked very beautiful.

"If you'll bring Puttyboy," Buttonsson called, as he took the Infanta by the hand and started away into the wood. "We're already behind. Winter-Hwen is going to be sad."

Rustass appeared puzzled. "Winter-Hwen!" he repeated a few times to himself. "Haven't I heard that name somewhere before?"

"Yup, plup, bluckle-lup!" said a musical voice beside his left shoe. It was Puttyboy, making plopping noises out of the sides of his head.

Rustass bent to gather him. Then started back in surprise. Puttyboy was growing up. Or something. At any rate he had changed. His outer coating seemed clearer and not so thick. His eyes were nearer the surface, still blue, but smaller and more lively. They were smiling. Rustass could also see definite signs of a nose and a mouth and a couple of ears. And way down there beneath the belt of the sacking skirt there appeared to be a tummy and perhaps even two little legs.

"Come on then," Rustass said. He took Puttyboy and placing him under his arm crossed the stream and climbed the far bank. He looked this way and that through the trees. The whole wood was clamouring in the wind. There was no sign of Buttonsson and the Infanta.

"Now where did those two go?" Rustass said aloud to himself.

"If you can't follow your nose," said a voice behind him, "try squinting down your tail. Then walk backwards. Haw-haw-haw!"

Rustass swung round. There was no one there. But he was in time to see the otter's shiny black tail, with one flip, disappear beneath the surface of the pool.

"Let's go, Puttyboy," Rustass muttered. "As if I didn't know the way by now."

He started to climb through the wood in the direction of the Bartons' big field. But, whether or no it was the wind, or some other reason, the wood today seemed all back to front. Instead of getting thinner and lighter, it appeared to get thicker and deeper.

And then quite suddenly something very odd happened. The wood got very much thicker and very much lighter at the same time.

And then Rustass stepped with Puttyboy out into a glade where he'd certainly never been before. The trees around the glade grew close together, and the day was dim, and yet the glade was light—a blue frosty light. The light seemed to be coming from one end of the glade, from half-way up a big oak tree.

"Ah, there you are," said Buttonsson. He was standing in the middle of the glade beside the Infanta. "Just in time. Winter-Hwen is ready to begin."

"Begin what?" Rustass asked nervously.

"Begin to tell you his story. Hold out your hand. Winter-Hwen, this is Mr Rustass."

Rustass suddenly felt it grow cold. He noticed too that the light had moved from the oak tree and was now all about him. Then Rustass felt someone take his hand and shake it.

"BRRRRRR!" Rustass shivered.

"It's quite true," said a strange, sad voice that wavered and whistled like an arctic wind over an ice-flow, "I do have cold hands."

"But," said the Infanta loftily, looking through Rustass as if he were a recaptured prisoner whose fate was altogether too unimportant for her to consider, "Winter-Hwen happens to have a warm heart. Besides, he's royalty. Like ourself."

"Yes, I do have a warm heart," said the cold voice.

"He'd need it," Rustass muttered. He was still trying to breathe warmth back into his fingers.

"And now," said Buttonsson, "he's going to tell you his story."

"Would he mind," Rustass said quickly, "going back up in his tree. I'd hate him to have a frosty reception."

The Infanta sniffed and turned her back on Rustass with a toss of her black hair.

"Thank you," said Winter-Hwen, a trifle coldly. "As it happens, when I recite my saga I prefer to sit."

The light moved back to the oak tree. Half way up.

"Years later," Winter-Hwen began, his thin voice wavering and failing like the music of wind in a hollow tree, "the blood-letting came to an end. Then the earth-mounds were swollen with the bones of many brave battle-warriors. Sikurd lay dead, he who had avenged Tikel Sigfusson, slain by Hrapp in the feud with Mord Kollskeg which arose out of the murder of Snorri Fiddle by the treacherous sons of Lambi Solmundarsson who had stolen the ancient war-axe, Lungsplitter, from Gunnar and Grim Night-Sun. Death is proud to have such heroes in his ale-hall."

"Oh dear," the Infanta yawned, "there he goes, name-dropping again. As if that sort of thing would impress *us*!"

"But then, years later," Winter-Hwen continued, "word came to Svinafell at the end of summer. Somewhere to the South and East a child had been born. A star marked his birth. Some said he was born a great hero. It was rumoured that his father was a better king than any other, a better protector, more generous with gifts. It was suggested that only the bravest could be ruled by him, those who carried tribute, rings and an ancient sword, to the cow-stall where his son had been born.

"Earl Ogmund was my father. He heard this. This was his reply:

"'It matters to me not the least bit if I die tomorrow, or some other time, so long as I die bravely. Loose the sail on my ship, Wolf-fang-raider. If the fates allow...'"

Buttonsson held up his hand.

"Just a second," he said. "This Wolf-fang-raider—*did* he loose the sail on the ship?"

"I'm sorry," said Winter-Hwen, "I should have made that clear. No, Wolf-fang-raider *was* the ship."

"That's what I thought," Buttonsson said. "And that's two ships. So we've still got a chance."

"But The Galleon was *first*," the Infanta pointed out. "Still never mind. You may carry on."

"Now where was I?" said Winter-Hwen. "Oh yes, Earl Ogmund's reply: 'Loose the sail on my ship. If my luck is good and the fates allow, I shall give the Warrior-Child my sword, Strong-tooth, which when danger is near gleams like frost at full-moon. We sail today. I will take with me my son Winter-Hwen.'

"We sailed South, encountering many storms. That year winter came with sharp teeth.

"In November Glum Unruly was killed by an Irish arrow. The same night the herald sang this song:

"'It has been a great Battle. The poet, when he sings of it, will earn mead in the hall. Gold for gold.

The warriors from the North were generously received by the Irish. Strong-tooth shone for three hours.

Brave men fell as Fate allotted. But of Norse men only Glum the Unruly. His oar will be missed.

Earl Ogmund's son showed no fear. He embroidered four Irish tunics with feathers.'

"That was I, Winter-Hwen, of course. The feathers were goose feathers, on the ends of my arrows.

"Wolf-fang-raider continued, his stern always towards the star that does not move. Soon he encountered a great storm.

"For several days the sky and the sea were one howl. There was none of the men who ever expected to see land again. On the seventh evening Strong-tooth began to gleam with a blue light. Earl Ogmund said:

" 'Since all this time Strong-tooth has not considered the sea dangerous, I take it we must be near land. I can't tell whether this is a good sign or not. But I wouldn't be surprised if the Storm Witch weren't at the back of it.'

"He had no sooner finished saying this when Wolf-fang-raider was thrown onto rocks. Immediately the wind dropped and the sea grew calm. The seafarers then saw that they were not far from the shore, beneath a line of looming cliffs."

"I expect it was Gallantry Beacon," Buttonsson whispered, "where Puttyboy came ashore."

"You mean," the Infanta said distantly, "where *we* came ashore. Either way, it was Barton work, we'll be bound."

"Wolf-fang-raider's back was snapped," Winter-Hwen continued. His voice wavered and he clearly considered he was telling a very exciting saga. "But he did not immediately break in pieces. Earl Ogmund looked at the black calm sea and the snouting rocks, and wondered whether to order the Norsemen to swim for the shore.

" 'Zwim today or zwim tomorrow,' an unpleasant voice called from half way up the cliff, 'bayn't that much difference, bwoys. You'll zwim directly, you'll zee.' "

"What did we tell you?" the Infanta said in a loud whisper. "Barton work!"

"And that proves it was Gallantry Beacon," Buttons-son said excitedly. "And *that* proves that we've found the second ship. Though where Summer Sun is, I'm not quite sure. Still just wait till Nossno hears about this—he'll go into orbit!"

"Nossno may be pleased," said Winter-Hwen sadly. "But this is a sad saga because when the Norsemen looked up at the cliffs, there, seated on ledges, were six large men, or trolls maybe, all alike. They were painted with blue paint, wore grizzly bear rugs, and carried great clubs. Also they had small red eyes, and red whiskers on the back of their necks. There was a seventh figure, similar to the others in all respects, except that for some reason it seemed probable she was a woman—of sorts.

"Earl Ogmund thought for a minute. Then, holding Strong-tooth firmly in his hand, he made this speech—which was, as it turned out, his last.

"'It seems to me that our voyage has not ended happily. I cannot doubt that the person on the cliffs is either the Storm-Witch, or else her rival in power and malice. If now by death I am prevented from seeing the birth-place of the Warrior-Child, I trust his Father will find place for me in his hall, on one of the mead-benches. If the feasting there is not excellent, I have come a long way for no great thing. Never in my sight has Strong-tooth gleamed more brightly than now. Since we are in such great danger I entrust to my son, Winter-Hwen, this ancient sword. I promise that none shall harm him, nor shall the light of Strong-tooth fail him, until he has laid the sword at the feet of the Warrior-Child. Not till that day shall Winter-Hwen return to our earldom in the North.'

"Earl Ogmund handed Strong-tooth to Winter-Hwen.

Then with a great war-cry he jumped into the sea and began to swim to the shore. All his men followed him.

"Immediately the sea grew tricky with currents. The black began to flash with the silver bodies of the evil Finn-folk. Very few of the seafarers reached the shore. And when any that did tried to get a hold on a rock, one of the six trolls would stamp on his fingers. He then fell back in the sea and was drowned or snatched by the Finn-folk.

"Winter-Hwen however was protected by Strong-tooth. The powerful light seemed to carry him over the waves. He found himself sitting alone very sad on a rock under the cliffs. The six trolls howled at him and waved their clubs in the air. But Strong-tooth's light seemed to trouble their red little eyes, and clearly they were afraid to come near.

"Then the Storm-Witch, or whoever it was, called to Winter-Hwen from her ledge half way up the cliff. This is what she said:

" 'Yer's a how-to, if ever 'twas. You'm all right just so long's ever thickee zord keeps shinning. But thickee zord bayn't goin' to shin unless you'm in danger, mind. That's the zum of it what your varther zed. 'E's shinning now, bwoy, because you'm in mortal danger—vrom us. But you once go away, he'll stop shinning, an' then I reckon you'm bound to come to 'arm. Best then bide 'ere with us zafe and zound where it's terrible dangerous. What d'ye say?'

"Never mind what Winter-Hwen had to say, the six trolls jigged and bristled their red whiskers and waved their clubs until the cliffs threatened to tumble. At length Winter-Hwen managed to make himself heard.

" 'It seems to me,' he said sadly, 'that I'd do better to go at once in search of the Warrior-Child. If fate allows that I find him, then that day, as spake the Earl my father, I can return home. I do not think I will fail to be well received.'

"'Mercy no, bwoy! Uz let'ee out of good mortal danger to where 'ee might come to 'arm. What doo'ee take us vor, then? Bartons? Tee-hee-hee. Tell'ee what uz'll do, though. You'll 'ave need of your legs drectly, when you come across that vine, brave bwoy you'm after—to get you 'ome. Zo us'll 'ave'em bide 'ere with uz—out of 'arm's way. Come to think of it, uz'd better take the 'ole body. Then uz'll be sure you'm zafe, then you.'

"Just then there was an arrow of lightning, and a rending of thunder. The last of Wolf-fang-raider slipped beneath the sea. And by the same black magic the body of Winter-Hwen was snatched from him. He had become invisible. Now no one could tell where he was—unless of course it happened that Strong-tooth was glowing. And that of course would only happen when Winter-Hwen was in serious danger. The Storm-Witch had worked a mean spell."

Winter-Hwen had been so caught up in his own saga that he'd begun to sound quite cheerful. But now he paused for breath, which may have been a mistake because when he continued he not only sounded sad again, but really tragic.

"Since that hour it has been my fate endlessly to remain in these woods. Each time I'm tempted to wander away, then very soon I am out of danger. Then immediately Strong-tooth's light vanishes. And there is nothing left of Winter-Hwen. I do not hold the chances of finding the Warrior-Child in these woods to be good. It is not always easy to detect the intentions of Fate.

"That's my saga. Now I suggest you take note of

how bright the light of Strong-tooth has suddenly become. Ssh! Listen!"

ErrrrrrrUMMMMMMMMMM rmmmm rmmmm
                        RMMMMMMMMMMMMMMMMMM

ErrrrrrrrrrrMMMMMMMMM. . . . .rm. . .rm. . . .rm. . . .
                                   rm. . . . .RR

ErrrrrrUmmmmMMMMMMMMMM Rmmmmm
                Rmmmm. . . . . . .ErRRRRR. . . . . .

ErrrrrrmmmmmmmmmmmmmmmMMMMMMMMMM
                     RR RR ErRRR. . .

RUMERUMERUMERUMERUM. . . .RRRR RUM

. . . .mmmmmmmmmmmmmmmmeRRRRRRRRRRRRRR
              RRRR. . . .RRRRMMMMMMMMMMM

Six triggerings of fearsome noise—all at once.

"Oh dear," said the Infanta loftily, "what a bore. If they find ourself we may be sure we'll never be able to walk in the woods again."

"Then I suggest you come and stand under this tree," Winter-Hwen said.

The Infanta and Rustass hesitated a moment. Then they walked towards the tree. Strong-tooth's gleam was now very bright indeed. As they entered the circle of light it became cold. And the next moment they found they had disappeared entirely from view.

"Thankyou," said the Infanta.

"Well," Winter-Hwen replied, "I did give your father my word that I'd *try* to look after you."

"Don't worry," Buttonsson called, "Puttyboy and me will take care of this."

"Puttyboy and *I*," the Infanta from somewhere within

the light corrected him sternly. "But," she added as the Bartons entered the glade, "he *is* rather brave."

"VOO-ALOOO!" yelled the Bartons above the barking of the dogs and the braying of the chain-saws.

Buttonsson waited while they thundered towards him up the glade. When they were close he turned and, with Puttyboy in his arms, trotted away into the wood.

The Bartons, without a blink in the direction of Strong-tooth's protective light, crashed after him.

"He's really *very* brave," the Infanta decided. "Think, if he'd a drop of royal blood in his veins, we might have chosen him as our. . ."

Maybe her voice was soft. Or maybe simply it was fading. Maybe it was fading in the same way that the light had begun to fade. Or as the crashing of the Bartons was now fading into the distance among the trees.

Fading, and gradually fading.

Rustass gave his head a good shake.

There he was, in the dusk, outside the cottage, looking down into this small parcel of sky. Or rather, now that he saw more exactly, into the pale blue of Buttonsson's eyes. All the pictures had gone.

"By the way," Buttonsson was saying, "Nossno's got to hear about your invention. He wants to know more about it. Will it be any *help*?"

Rustass hesitated—then he smiled.

"I should have thought," he said, "that this Nosmo. . ."

"Noss*no*."

". . .that this Nossno, not that I've ever had the privilege of meeting him, would be able to *see* my invention. As it is I'm afraid he'll have to wait."

"When will it be finished?" Buttonsson asked eagerly.

"Maybe," said Rustass with the satisfied expression of someone who feels he's getting his own back, "by Christmas."

Buttonsson thought for a minute. Then changed the subject.

"It's good that we've found *two* ships. But the real problem is going to be the third. Nossno says he hasn't a clue about the third. Without that we're sunk—specially after what happened today. Now the Bartons are really sore. Nossno says there's no longer any way out: Christmas will be the showdown. One way or the other. Quite frightening really."

At that moment from far away, from the gloom beyond the woods, came the sulky mutter of a chain-saw. Rustass chuckled.

"There goes Barton. . .excuse me. There go the Bartons stomping home. Which reminds me: where did you get to?"

"Oh," said Buttonsson, "I thought you had *seen*."

"Well, I did *nearly*, but it was rather dark. So perhaps you'd be good enough to put me in the picture."

Buttonsson grinned up at him. His eyes were the brightest thing left in the day.

"All right," he said, "but this could be the last time."

Rustass, all at once, found he was walking in the wind up the path to the cottage. He was on his way back from the meeting with Winter-Hwen.

"Brrrrrrh!" he said, hugging himself as he walked. "Talk about cold company—my bones are still aching like icicles!"

But at that moment he stopped and swung round. He

thought he had heard in some close pocket of the wind a distant muttering. He shielded his eyes with both cupped hands, and looked across the valley.

There along the bottom of the field towards the sea ran Buttonsson. He was holding Puttyboy in both arms. They must have broken through the hedge from the lane at the top of the wood. They ran a hundred yards and then stopped and looked back.

'Im's-Jack's was first through the hedge. He fell on his nose, heavily. Even at that distance, Rustass saw him open his big mouth to yowl. But whether he did yowl or no became a mystery in the wind. Then came Dan with his chain-saw held high in the air and 'im's-Len's between his legs dragging at Len who was grabbing at Jan to keep his balance and save him from falling back on Sam's chain-saw which had become snagged in 'im's-Stan's leash and dragged from his clutch onto the ground where it had started to race around like a mad thing, trimming 'im's-Dan's tail as it went and cutting a hole in Dan's boot. Jack was last through the hedge, hugging his huge chain-saw so close to his furious purple face it looked as if he were trying to give the orange bristles on his chin a fine shave.

Six Bartons, six chain-saws—and not a sound. The gale took care of that.

Buttonsson and Puttyboy watched the Bartons form up in the field, line abreast. Rustass, even at that distance, and through the gloomy twilight, saw Jack Barton's jaw shudder. That was him giving the command. The Bartons, well-drilled, lowered their chain-saws to the level of Buttonsson's knees. And charged.

Buttonsson watched the charge until it was two parts of the way to him. Then he turned with Puttyboy and trotted on along the bottom of the field towards the sea. Suddenly he stopped. He was beside the gap in the hedge made that same summer by the beeline of Jan's tractor, and by Jan hitched by his belt to its tow-bar, on their way down the hill and through the gorse patch and into the stream. Buttonsson hesitated. He glanced back at the Bartons, who were breathing hard behind him. Then he turned down the hill, into the gorse patch, after Jan's tractor. Which was a mistake.

The first twenty yards down into the gorse patch Buttonsson made good speed. Then two things happened. The Bartons arrived at the gap in the hedge and stood in a panting line looking down. And Buttonsson discovered that from this point in the tractor's trail the gorse had recovered and so had the brambles and much of the bracken.

When they looked down and saw Buttonsson and Puttyboy hindered by the undergrowth a smile twisted down the line of the Bartons from end to end. Then all together they shouted:

"HA-HA!"

and they must have shouted very loud because Rustass, even on the other side of the valley, caught a whisper of the sound through all that length of the gale.

The Bartons set their dogs at heel, well out of the way of the whizzing chains. Like one huge cutter with six sharp blades they started forward down into the gorse patch.

Buttonsson was forced to scramble to make headway. The gorse scratched at him, the old bracken held him by the ankles, and the brittle autumn brambles clicked and giggled as they clawed him back. He and Puttyboy were unable to move as fast as he would have liked.

But the Bartons came steadily down the hill, cutting

a clean swathe through the gorse patch. They made better progress than Buttonsson.

Rustass on the other side of the valley growled and clenched his fists. But he still held his hands in front of his eyes; and so he had to unclench his fists again in order to see what was happening to Buttonsson.

Buttonsson tripped. He rolled several yards down the hill, which was a help. But ended in a gorse bush with a branch hooked under his denim jacket.

"VOO-ALOOO, BWOYS," screamed Jack, and all the Bartons revved their saws to a scream which Rustass, all that way down the gale, heard like the whine of a hungry mosquito.

The Bartons came steadily on. Buttonsson wriggled again. He was almost free, but there were only nine feet between him and the screech of the nearest saw.

The distance was shrinking. It was down to five feet.

Rustass took his hands away from his eyes. Suddenly he could hear the Bartons' chain-saws as if they were at work on the inside of his own head. What had happened was this: a new lull in the gale had come. The valley was absolutely still. And silent. In fact everything seemed all at once to be holding its breath as if suddenly it were listening to the chain-saws' deadly song.

With a terrific shout, the cock pheasants all got up together. In fact it seemed to Rustass, though he was too far away to see for certain, that one by one they flew out of Buttonsson's boots.

They flew up the hill straight at the Bartons. The Bartons ducked—in fact so fast that they only just didn't cut off their six heads with their chain-saws. Then they were on their backs with their feet in the air, and the saws were waving around like huge thistles on the feeble stalks of their arms.

This is what had happened. The dogs had been gollopping patiently along at heel behind the Bartons. Until all of a sudden six fat cock pheasants had gone low overhead. Too much for any dog, and each had heaved back on the leash as he flung himself in pursuit up the hill. It was this that brought the Bartons down.

Buttonsson bent double with laughter, and that freed him finally from the gorse bush. So then he turned and scrambled on down the hill, across the stream and up into the field on the other side. There he appeared to wait for the Bartons to catch up. Which they hurried to do just as soon as ever they could get to their feet.

"Don't hang around," Rustass muttered urgently, and began to clench his fists all over again.

But Buttonsson did hang around. In fact for a moment it seemed he was going to offer the Bartons a hand up the bank out of the stream. He didn't though. He just turned and strolled across the field as if there were no worry in the world.

"Get a move on," Rustass yelled.

But there was something he had forgotten. And the Bartons had overlooked.

Rustass, glaring down the valley over the trees, saw in the dusk the whole pack of Bartons go into the stream, and come out at full cry on the near bank. Now for the kill, and they and their dogs and their chainsaws bayed as they chased the last few yards after Buttonsson.

Buttonsson stopped in his tracks.

"HA-HA," yelled the Bartons.

"Good evening, Mr Brewer," Buttonsson called out, cheerfully.

There they all were in Mr Brewer's field.

Jan was the leading Barton. He pulled up short as if his muscles had snapped. Len was next, his saw went roaring into Jan's backside. Then Stan; his saw screamed into Len. Dan's into Stan. Sam's into Dan. And finally Jack, his saw tore a strip out of Sam. The dogs thought their masters were having a scrap. So they joined in too, baring their rotten teeth and slashing at anything that moved. Until:

"Good evening," said Mr Brewer politely.

There he was, up a ladder on the roof of his dutch barn, tying ropes to stop the gale, should it return, from blowing away with his corrugated iron. The last chain-saw muttered into silence.

"Not a bad sort of an evening," Mr Brewer said quietly, as he eyed the Bartons.

The Bartons bravely were trying to smile, and not to blubber, and at the same time were bowing and raising their caps. And their dogs were grinning guiltily and wagging their tails. They were all—the men and the dogs—doing everything in their power to behave themselves. But at the same time they were snarling under their breath and rubbing their backsides, and longing only for a chance to biff or bite each other in the eye or the leg.

"Master strong wind," Jack Barton said, and "Might 'ave a touch of vrost drectly."

"Well, I must get home to my tea," Buttonsson said as he walked to the gate of the field. "Goodbye Mr Brewer. Goodbye Mr Barton."

"Goodbye me buddivul," said Mr Barton with a smile like a bad wound, and all his sons waved, and kicked their dogs to remind them to grin—sickeningly.

"Look!" said Buttonsson.
Rustass opened his eyes.

Buttonsson was holding Puttyboy up so that Rustass could get a close look at his face. Rustass appeared to start—there was something the matter with Puttyboy's glass eye. It seemed to be made up of hundreds of small black eyes that were made up of hundreds of tiny black eyes—all shining.

"Now he really will need the oculist," Rustass gasped.

But Buttonsson simply pushed past him and opened the front door.

"Mum," he called, "please may Puttyboy come in if he wipes his feet. He's brought you a present."

"Dear soul, of course he can," Nancy smiled to him over her shoulder from the stove. "A present for me! He do know how to please a maid. Do I keep it till Christmas?"

"Oh no. There may not *be* a Christmas this year."

"Why ever not indeed? Blackberries! Thankyou, Mr Puttyboy. Just for that you can sit up to the table. See what I've been doing this afternoon? Made *him* a present. A special cushion."

"Blackberries," Rustass repeated to himself, as he came in and closed the front door behind him. He was looking quite relieved. "So he did keep *one* eye open!"

Outside in the valley night fell, and the wind once again started to blow.

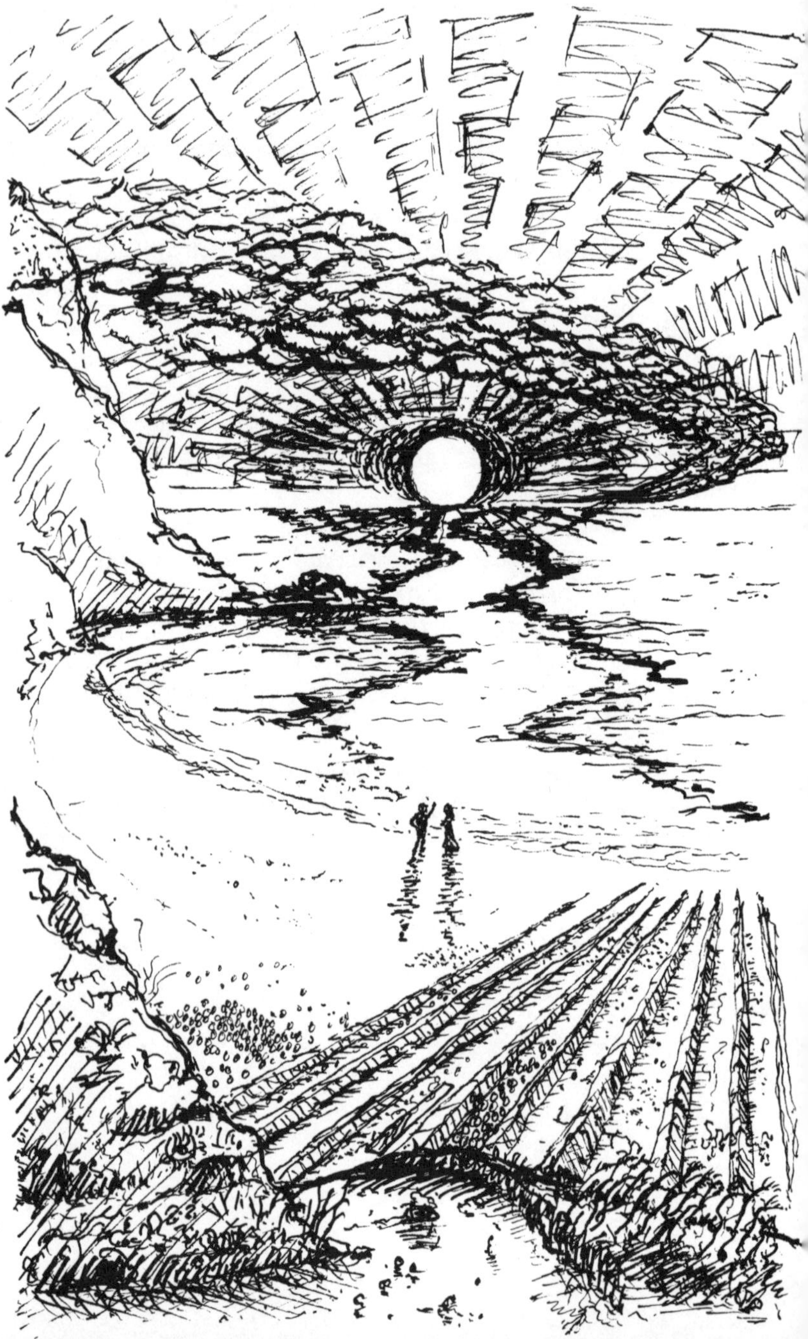

WINTER

It was Christmas Eve.

Rustass stood outside the front door of the cottage and listened. Which was what Buttonsson (at lunchtime) had told him was what Nossno had said he should do.

As he listened he watched the golden winter light drain to the west and fade. He felt the recoil of the sap in the grass. And he sensed the numbness in the earth as the frost settled, and then began to tighten its grip.

Then for some reason he looked up, and was exactly in time to see the shivering diamond point of the first star.

And all the time he was listening, through and across and aslant the complete stillness, for some move by the Bartons.

Or just for the first sound. But we'll come back to that...

For one reason or another Rustass had been *seeing* THE Bartons all day. They'd been busy. Busy with their harrows first thing. Shortly after breakfast Rustass had seen them harrowing across their big field above Mr Brewer's field across the valley, hard on the skipping heels of Buttonsson as he ran for it with Puttyboy in his arms. And just before lunch they had been out with their six muck-spreaders in the big field. Rustass, growling and clenching his fists, had watched, had actually seen the muck fly as they hurtled down the hill after Buttonsson and Puttyboy. 'Im's-Jack's, 'im's-Jan's, 'im's-Dan's, 'im's-Sam's, 'im's-Stan's, and 'im's-Len's had gollopped along behind happy as pigs in the shower of muck. Buttonsson had leapt through the hedge into the gorse patch in the nick of time. The Bartons had piled their tractors up in the hedge with a jolt that threw the muck forward out of the spreaders on top of Jack, Dan, Sam, Stan and Len. They had looked like a line of steaming dung-stooks. Not Jan though. His tractor had gone straight through the hedge, straight on down through the great gorse patch, straight over the bank and with a splash straight into the stream. And the jolt threw the muck forward out of the spreader on top of him: a steaming dung-stook in the middle of the stream.

"Bartons have been busy," Rustass mentioned as Buttonsson came up the path for his lunch.

Buttonsson stopped. In fact he took a step backward.

"Did you really?" he asked excitedly. "I mean, did you *see* them?"

Rustass looked down at his great hands, modestly. And said nothing.

"Yes, they have been busy," Buttonsson said at length. "But not so busy as they're going to be. Nossno's pretty certain that the showdown's coming this evening."

He turned, and for a moment stared out at the sea which was calm and pale grey, the colour of bonfire ash. And empty.

Buttonsson shook his head.

"Still no sign," he said. "It's getting serious."

"I did see one ship this morning," said Rustass. "But it sailed past."

They went into the cottage.

"You'll be going out again this afternoon, I expect," Nancy said to Buttonsson when they were eating their lunch.

"Yes, I'm afraid so. Puttyboy's got an appointment."

Nancy looked at Rustass and winked.

"I've not bothered with any old decorations," she said, "because *some*-body told me there might not be a Christmas this year."

"I know," said Buttonsson vaguely. He appeared to be thinking of something else.

At the end of the meal Buttonsson jumped down from his chair and picked Puttyboy up from his.

"Sorry we can't stop. Mustn't be late."

"Just a second," Rustass said. "What's the matter with Puttyboy's head?"

"Nothing much. He's growing a horn. Nossno says it's the one good sign."

He held Puttyboy up for Rustass to examine. Rustass looked closely.

"I see," he said. Which wasn't exactly true, because what it seemed to him he saw was a coil of old ram's horn stuck into a ball of very old tallow.

"What time's the appointment?" Rustass then asked.

"You'll see. Nossno says to count seven after the first star."

"Seven of what?"

"Seven sounds. Then see if there's another. Goodbye."

"You'll not be late for your supper Master Buttonsson, I trust," Nancy called after him.

"What, be late for my Christmas pudding! The Bartons would need to have cut off my legs."

He then closed the door behind him, and Nancy and

Rustass heard him laugh to himself grimly as he ran down the path.

Rustass spent the short cold afternoon putting the finishing touches to his invention. He oiled the gears, greased the bearings and repointed the points. He then cut kindling for the fire from boxwood washed up last summer at Wagwater Mouth. He sawed logs from oak branches fallen in the woods after the autumn gales. And finally, with the daylight already hurrying out of the woods, he axed out the stump of an old apple tree and carved it to the length of the hearth—the yule-log to carry the fire through Christmas.

But all the time he worked he was listening, through and across and aslant the dreaming stillness of the winter afternoon, for some sound from Farmer Barton.

There was no sound.

And yet Rustass sensed that for all the silence there was business afoot in the woods. There was an edge to the silence. A watchfulness. When the single raven started up and flapped over the valley he croaked just twice—as if he too had noticed how, at the still point where all the silence was gathered, fear was on the move.

Rustass put the axe away in the woodshed round the back of the cottage. Then, carrying his invention in a clean sack, he returned and took up his position by the front door.

The thin light was suddenly golden, thrown back from the gleaming sunset out over the sea. Rustass stamped to keep the blood moving in his toes, and the metal bits to his heels rang on the frosted iron-stone earth.

Then for some reason he looked up, and was exactly in time to see the shivering point of the first star.

He had been listening all the time, but now he began to listen very attentively.

THE SEVEN SOUNDS

His ears had become so tuned to silence that it took them some time to register the first sound. Then they caught it. A fizzing noise, like fine bubbles surfacing on a pond. It was his own breath falling on the freezing air. He counted one.

He counted two, marking the score by catching two fingers on his left hand in the fist of his right. That was when he heard Nancy busy in the kitchen. In her clear happy voice she had begun to sing.

This was her song:

> *The wind has moved North*
> *Its teeth are laid bare*
> *I searched the garden*
> *Found nobody there*
> *The robin last evening*
> *Cheeped autumn's song*
> *But this morning the raven*
> *And he has gone.*

As if it needed to answer the song, a robin somewhere in the wood nearby piped faintly three or four times. Rustass grabbed another finger. He counted three.

It was some time before he heard the fourth sound. But when suddenly it dawned on him he realized he'd been listening to it all along. The stream from the depth of the valley. On and on it went with its cold spellbound patter, as if making the case that its sound *was* a helping of silence—only served in a richer measure.

"That makes four," said Rustass and helped himself to another finger.

His thumb made five. That was when over the wood and across one meadow Mr Brewer in his shippon turned on the machine for the evening milking. A drowsy sound, like a mechanical cat purring beside an electric fire. For a moment Rustass fancied he smelt the hay and the steaming cows, and he wondered what shape stirred in a cow's memory that told her of Christmas Eve.

He switched hands quickly, the left fingers to count, the right to be counted.

Six.

Or was he mistaken?

He let go the finger.

He seized it again.

Now his ear could hold the sound. A clear waver of bells. The marvellous change was faint, yet all of it reached him over the frozen, listening earth, from somewhere miles inland. Rustass held his breath. He narrowed his eyes and nodded his head in time to the distant chime.

Then Rustass was upright, alert. His head moved sharply as he looked about him. Had there been a sound, a seventh sound? Or had it been his fancy, or perhaps a bone-crick inside him?

He listened.

Maybe, that was it, maybe he was alive to the echo before the sound, the flinch in the silence.

Then the crash came.

Clear as if it broke at the bottom of the garden, a single huge wave slumped onto the beach, ran at the cliff, dragging the pebbles with a deep grovelling noise, seemed to swallow, and finally slunk back into the sea.

One wave, on Christmas Eve, out of a calm sea. Then silence.

"Seven," Rustass whispered, as if afraid everything might shatter if he added the least noise. It was then he remembered that this was the hour of Puttyboy's appointment.

But was it seven, or was it to be eight sounds? Rustass breathed some warmth into his fingers, then put his hands in his pockets and continued to listen.

When he first heard the eighth sound he thought he must have gone round in a circle, and be back where he started. He thought it was his breath again fizzing on the frosty air. But then he realized the fizzing was more brittle, more as if a sparkler were being waved in a closed room. But there was music to it too: a fine, distant wavering music, like the sound of a moist finger-tip drawn round the rim of a thin wine-glass.

Rustass walked a few paces down the path. He put his hands on his hips and leaned back and looked up at the comet.

The comet appeared three times as large as the largest star, and quarter the size of the moon. It was flickering blue, the colour of flame on a frosty night. And it wore its sparkling tail wrapped round it like the trailer on a Catherine Wheel. Where was it off to? That was the point, this solid bit of the sky didn't seem so much in flight as to hover, turning slowly—a few turns this way, then a few turns that way, its tail winding and unwinding in an undecided manner. Or else in a decided manner.

The comet turned.
Rustass blinked.
The comet came to rest, then began to turn the other way.

Rustass rubbed the light out of his eyes with his huge fists, and looked again.

No doubt about it—pictures had begun to figure in the eye of the comet.

One in particular.

Rustass slipped on the old wet leaves. But he managed with one hand to grab hold of the oak branch above his head. Otherwise he'd certainly have slid with his precious sack into the pool beneath the waterfall.

The grey heron had been standing on one leg at the edge of the pool like a forgotten umbrella. Now he gathered himself into the air and with silent scorn turned his back on Rustass and flapped away upstream. He looked like a handful of tatters and dry kindling sticks knocked flying by the wind.

"It's so good of you to be late," the Infanta said icily. "We ourself have enjoyed standing here freezing to death. Not that royalty feels the cold."

She looked down on Rustass from the bank on the far side of the stream, as if he were a distant glimpse of the castle of a rather poor relation. She was wearing a cocked hat, muff and long coat of brown sable, trimmed and lined with crimson sheep-skin. She looked very beautiful, and extremely cold.

Buttonsson, chuckling, jumped to his feet. He'd been sitting on the bank beside the Infanta.

"What's colder than the eyes of the Queen of Castile?" he called.

Rustass had begun to scratch his head and to look awkwardly at his boots when he heard a sad wavering voice.

"Oh, not again," said Winter-Hwen, sounding like a cold draft in a belfry. "It seems to me less than fair to go on and on making up riddles about my condition."

He must have been standing quite close to Rustass because Rustass shivered.

"What have you got there?" the Infanta asked with an imperious wave of her hand in the direction of Rustass's sack.

"That," Buttonsson said quickly, as if to help Rustass who, he knew, would be tongue-tied, "is his latest invention. It hasn't been unveiled yet. But he's a terrific inventor. It'll be useful, you can be sure of that."

The Infanta inclined her head, and her red mouth narrowed in a thin superior smile.

"Could you bring Puttyboy," Buttonsson shouted to Rustass. Then he added in a loud whisper, "Winter-Hwen will show you the way. There's no time to lose."

With that, he took the Infanta by the hand and set off down the bank of the stream in the direction of the sea.

"Where *is* Puttyboy?" Rustass muttered, as he looked across the stream and here and there among the trees.

"Mind you don't step on him," Winter-Hwen called from somewhere close by. "He looks over-ripe to me, as if he might go plop anytime."

Rustass looked down. There was Puttyboy right beside his foot. He hadn't been there a moment before. Rustass bent and picked him up. But then when he saw what was happening he nearly dropped him again. Winter-Hwen was right. Puttyboy did look as if he might go plop. His surface was as taut as a pig's bladder stoked with lard. And there, deep inside yet clearly visible, the innards were churning. Those blue watery eyes, little hands, feet, tummy and bottom—turning over and over like a baby gone for a spin in a tumble-drier.

"I think we should hurry," Winter-Hwen's voice

sounded. "You may not have noticed but my sword, Strong-tooth, has begun to glow. That means danger is approaching."

As Rustass set out with Puttyboy towards the sea, following in the twilight the cold blue glow, he heard in the woods behind and on both sides of them heavy breathing, and the scrunch of farm boots on the frosted leaves. And now and then in the deepening gloom he would see the smoulder of a pair of little red eyes.

When they reached the cliff above Wagwater Mouth they stopped for a moment. Twenty yards behind them in the gloom the little red eyes stopped too.

But Rustass never glanced back. He was looking down at the beach. The sea was far out, beyond the ribs of rock, beyond the great sweep of sand. It was grey-green and smooth as the leaf of a leek. The red sun that moment settled on the horizon. Far away beneath them, where the sea lipped the sand, two small figures were standing side by side. Buttonsson and the Infanta.

Rustass heard Winter-Hwen sigh.

"Many have turned that great down-land with their sea-ploughs," he said. "It has not been made amply clear when fate will allow me to add my one northward furrow. But now let's be quick, or we'll be late."

"Late for what?" Rustass asked.

"That," Winter-Hwen said sadly, "is a poor riddle. When one is *late*, there is nothing to be late *for*. Come on."

Rustass, as he followed the glow down the cliff path, looked confused.

"Nossno said it would be at sunset," Buttonsson was saying.

He and the Infanta were standing side by side. They were watching the horizon so intently that they didn't appear to notice when Rustass and Puttyboy and the glow of Strong-tooth came and stood beside them.

"O," the Infanta replied loftily. "Funny, because he told *ourself* it would be when the tide turned."

"What would be?" Rustass asked.

They looked round at him for a second, the Infanta with disdain, as if Rustass were the end of a vanishing trick she'd seen any number of times before.

"You'll see," Buttonsson said, but quite gently, and he added behind his hand to the Infanta, "You know, he's much better at riddles than he used to be."

"We think," said the Infanta, "the tide is turning."

"Look!" shouted Buttonsson. "The sun is just going. Look, it's gone. Now."

But had it?

The horizon seemed to dip, and it appeared that a fraction of the sun reemerged. This spill flared—frosty blue. It parted from the sea-line. It took off on its own, flying in the face of the sky.

"Wow," said Buttonsson, "slap on time. But it's serious because it isn't a ship."

"What did Nossno say its name would be?" Winter-Hwen asked.

"Um. . ." said the Infanta and Buttonsson, trying to remember.

But Rustass felt Puttyboy shift in his arms. Very quietly Puttyboy made this strange plopping noise.

"Cattatoupek," said Rustass.

The Infanta looked at him sharply.

"And how did *you* know?" she demanded.

"A friend of mine told me," Rustass said carelessly.

"O," said the Infanta, and when she turned inquiringly

to Buttonsson she found he was smiling oddly as if he was pleased about something.

The comet came straight in at them over the sea. As it approached they heard its thin music and the distant crackle of the sparks in its tail. The sound grew louder, very eerie in the still evening. Then all at once they found they were listening to another noise—a low scything in the sea. They looked.

"Quick," yelled Buttonsson, "back up the beach!"

As Cattatoupek's glimmering reflection accelerated towards them over the still sea, so it seemed to take suddenly in tow a single immense wave. The wave made little noise, just this scything, and the occasional slop when the sea was overstretched and broke at the summit. It loomed larger.

"This should be far enough," Buttonsson said when they reached the top of the sand. They all turned and looked back.

The wave stretched from end to end of Wagwater Mouth. As it neared the sand the front side of the wave grew steeper, and more hollow. It could now be seen that it carried some black thing in its lap; it seemed to nurse it along, skimming it towards the shore over the surface of the sea.

"Could it be the ship?" yelled Buttonsson.

Two things happened.

Cattatoupek passed directly overhead in a fritter of sound like the sound of a flight of starlings. And the wave broke. It broke its entire length in one great smack. The fragments rushed and tumbled and hissed towards them. And as they came they nudged and nuzzled the black thing—whatever it was—up the beach.

"All we can say," said the Infanta, "is that this wave had better not wet *our* boots."

It didn't. The wave simply delivered the black thing—whatever it was—and then sank into the sand with a sigh.

They were all silent for a minute. Especially Rustass, because to him the black thing looked like nothing so much as an old wooden crate with Tel Aviv Fruit Co. printed on one side.

Winter-Hwen spoke:

"There are many heroes who would not eagerly set sail on the great Whale-road in such a ship," he said.

Buttonsson was clearly disappointed too.

"I suppose," he said, "Nossno could have made a mistake. Still we'll have to try and take it with us. Oh dear, what a pickle we're in, because Cattatoupek won't wait for us you know. How ever are we going to manage?"

"There's always my invention," said Rustass, modestly. "Would somebody kindly hold Puttyboy?"

The others then watched as Rustass took the sack from his shoulder and shook the shining pieces out onto the sand. Axles, aluminium slats, spark-plugs in a plastic bag, chassis-stays, wheels and wing-nuts. It was wonderful how nimbly Rustass's huge fingers went to work. In less than two minutes he'd assembled his invention.

"Wow!" said the Infanta.

"There! What did I tell you?" said Buttonsson proudly.

"You sit there at the front on the engine-cover," Rustass told the Infanta. "And Winter-Hwen beside you—the motor will keep him warm. Now, let's see. Yes, this box-thing can travel in the middle, with Puttyboy inside it. Buttonsson can sit on the back of the box...like that. And I," he said, stepping aboard over the back axle, and taking the steering-wheel in both hands, "I will drive."

Rustass pressed a button. The engine started.

"Follow that star," yelled Buttonsson.

And away they went up the beach.

At that moment down the cliff path came tripping and rolling and pitching a terrible troupe of Bartons all muddled with the pack of their dogs. They gathered speed as they went, until they fetched up suddenly at the foot of the cliffs in a biffing heap that squealed. And roared.

Before the Bartons could disengage themselves from each other and their dogs, the invention had coasted past. It seemed to take a deep breath, and then up it went, smoothly over the jagged stones.

"Olé," the Infanta called above the drilling of the engine. "We may after all have to find you a place in our government."

"Minister of Technology," said Rustass, and sounded the horn.

From behind came the sound of a different horn, and the terrible baying of men and dogs. The Bartons were back on their feet. Their blood was up. They followed for the kill.

Cattatoupek led the way. The invention, with its independent springing, motored smoothly beneath.

Because Buttonsson knew every dent in the ground he was able to tell Rustass where to steer. And when it became too dark for even him to be sure, they would simply wait for the Bartons to catch up a little—then Strong-tooth would glow like a fog-lamp, and the way would be clear.

They crossed the three low-lying meadows of Wag-water Farm, and the lane. They re-entered the oakwood and, with a fine splash, crossed the stream at a fording place not far from the waterfall. Still following Cattatoupek they motored in low-gear up the steep side of the valley, their way winding between the silent dreaming oak trees. So at length they reached the lane between the wood and the Bartons' big field.

Here the invention drew up. Cattatoupek had stopped in his tracks and was humming in an odd wavering way, as if in two minds. They could hear not far behind the crash and heave as the Bartons came panting after them through the undergrowth.

"I think the star's lost," said Rustass grimly.

"We don't," said the Infanta.

And with that Cattatoupek set off to the right. The invention followed down the lane.

Soon they came to the gate of Mr Brewer's other field. Buttonsson leapt down and opened the gate. Rustass drove through. Buttonsson shut the gate, and jumped back on board.

"I think I know where he's leading us," he said, as they drove along the hedge at the bottom of the field.

"If you don't, we do," said the Infanta.

She was cool and unruffled in her long fur coat.

At the bottom of Mr Brewer's field, over the hedge in the far corner, the two woods met. The oakwood of the valley and the sinister brooding firwood that ran up over the hill as far as the Bartons' farm. Both woods crowded in on the field, and it seemed that each tried to possess the corner with its own peculiar silence.

Now, in this corner there was an old shippon that belonged to Mr Brewer. It had a slate roof, an old oak door on a rusty hinge, and cob walls. The shippon would have fallen down centuries ago but for the strong enfolding ivy that held it together. Buttonsson knew the shippon well. He knew the barn-owls who lived there, and he visited them on summer evenings when they were ghosting the field at the start of a night's hunting.

Directly over this corner of the field, Cattatoupek halted. A second or two later the invention drove up. Rustass parked outside the old shippon in the blue half-light that shone from the comet. They all looked up.

"See," said Buttonsson, "you can tell he's stopped by the way he's got his tail wound round him."

"Like St. Catherine's wheel," said the Infanta. "Should we go in?"

"No, not quite yet," said Buttonsson.

The night was frosty, starlit and very still. In the distance, back in the oakwood they could hear the stomp and stumble of the Bartons, and their curses as they dragged behind them their bloated dogs. They heard them at the gate. Then it was silent. A minute later Strong-tooth's glow began to brighten. Then suddenly, in the farthest limit of his light, they saw the squinny and wink of twenty-four little red eyes: two greedy rows, six pairs to each.

"Now is the time," Buttonsson said.

He jumped down and pushed open the door of the shippon.

Rustass pressed the button. The engine started. And in they drove.

Strong-tooth's light fell on the old cobbled floor and the brown cobweb tapestries that swung from the slate-slats in the roof.

In the far corner a figure got to his feet. He'd been kneeling, studying a large plan by the light of a bicycle torch.

"I say," he said, "jolly well done. Splendid."

He appeared to be a boy of about fourteen, but very tall and thin. He was wearing grey flannel trousers, a white cricket shirt open at the neck, and a green tweed sports jacket. Behind his black horn-rimmed spectacles his brown eyes beamed out at them all in the most friendly way imaginable.

"My," he said, looking at the invention, "what a perfectly first-rate invention. Slap on time. Splendid."

"This is Rustass," said Buttonsson. "And this is Nossno."

"Jolly nice to meet you," said Nossno. "Heard lots about you. Good to have you on our side. A bit of a boffin, eh? First rate."

Rustass bowed his head modestly.

"Ah, what have we here?" Nossno asked, bending down to peer at the black box-thing.

"It's what the sea delivered," Buttonsson explained. "But I don't know if it's any use. It's not much of a ship."

"Not to worry," Nossno said. "Sure, it's just the ticket. Perhaps you, Rustass, would be good enough to put it over in that corner. By the way, how's our Puttyboy bearing up?"

"If his weight's anything to go by. . ." Rustass muttered, as he staggered with the box-thing over to the corner. "And he's begun to make odd noises."

Which was true. Puttyboy was making a noise rather like a baby with a pillow over its head, chortling to itself.

"We," the Infanta said definitely, "shall look after Puttyboy."

"Capital," said Nossno.

"I've never liked to spoil a good party," said Winter-Hwen gloomily. "But Strong-tooth appears a little unsettled."

Strong-tooth was flashing very brightly indeed, in blue menacing gleams.

"VOO ALOO BWOYS!" yelled Farmer Barton from out in the dark. "In us go!"

"I say, just a tick," said Nossno delightedly as he studied his plan. "Oh yes, that's it. Rustass, would you mind awfully closing the door?"

Rustass leapt to the door, slammed it, and put his great back against it.

Just in time.

THUD.

The door was hit by a whole heap of Bartons. For a moment there was silence. Then from outside came sounds of biffing and squealing.

Between Rustass's knees Buttonsson added his weight to the door.

"I say, *well* done," said Nossno. "First rate."

"I should love to be of use," Winter-Hwen said sadly. "I expect I'm quite heavy by now."

Silence—then the sound of several, say twelve, noses snuffling under and at the cracks of the door.

"Dawn'tee bother over much, you," Jack Barton called, "us'll 'ave 'ee drectly, you'll zee."

The snuffling ceased. But a moment later there were other noises. There was grabbing in the ivy and a scrabbling on the cob. From the base of the walls came a scuffling, digging sound. And from the roof there was thumping, and the shriek of stumpy finger-nails clawing at the slates. The Bartons were trying to find a way in.

"They're trying to find a way in," said Nossno, beaming round at each of them in turn. "Splendid."

Winter-Hwen went over beside the Infanta so that Strong-tooth's light shone all around her and the crate.

"I suppose you *must*," the Infanta said. "But I doubt

it's good for Puttyboy. You're too cold to be true!"

Winter-Hwen sighed.

Buttonsson, from between Rustass's knees, tilted his head and looked up at Rustass. He smiled broadly and winked.

"Well, Mr Rustass?" he said. "Now do you *see*?"

But before Rustass could reply, Nossno had finished consulting his plan, had glanced at his luminous wrist-watch, and was saying:

"Spot on. No problem at all. Now let's see what Mr Barton has to say."

And at that moment from out in the dark came a shout from Jack.

"Come 'ere bwoys. Us kin shiver thickee door with this-yer tree, I reckon. Then uz'll not go short for goose and figgy-pudden! Ha-ha!"

Outside the shippon there was the sound of squelching as the Bartons, man and dog, licked their lips.

"Vall to, bwoys," yelled Jack.

The Bartons grunted as they lifted the tree.

The dogs whined.

"Here they come," Nossno announced. "First rate. What a bun-fight, eh?"

The earth shook as the Bartons got up steam and thundered with their battering-ram down on the door.

Strong-tooth gleamed still brighter. In addition to his light, he now gave off a menacing whine.

THUMP PLOD. SPLOSH PLOD.

Rustass would do what he could. He closed his eyes and braced himself against the door, thrusting with his knees and his great shoulders.

Nossno took another quick look at the master-plan.

"I think we'll have you stand out of the way for this one, Rustass, if you don't mind," he said, his head forward and smiling at Rustass over the top of his horn-rims.

Rustass opened his eyes. He glanced at Buttonsson.

"Quick," said Buttonsson. "Out of the way."

Rustass scratched his head. He appeared confused.

"Quick," said Buttonsson. And then, "QUICKLY!"

Rustass shrugged his shoulders, and as he walked away so Nossno sauntered past him.

"*Splen*did," he said, and flung open the door.

In cantered the Bartons carrying a tree-trunk. Each Barton, expecting the shock as the tree hit the door, had his shoulders hunched and his head down and his eyes shut. It must have seemed to them as they ran with that weight that the door was a long time coming.

"Left-right. Left-right. Left-right," Nossno called out briskly.

The Bartons' hob-nails sparked in perfect time as they tripped over the cobbles of the shippon floor. Right across the shippon floor.

THUD.

The tree went straight through the cob wall on the far side of the shippon. It left a big hole. But not so big that the Bartons, charging neatly with their knees up and their heads down, failed to bruise themselves severely about their ears, their elbows and their shins as they followed through—and out again into the night and the hedge of the field and the ditch on the far side of the hedge. Their faithful dogs were, as ever, to heel. And by the sound of it they decided to get their teeth well stuck-in to the grumbling heap before the biffing began.

Had the danger passed? Strong-tooth appeared to consider it had. His light flickered and went out.

For a time no one moved in the shippon and the

only sound was the sound of Buttonsson laughing. And Nossno winding his watch.

But then something mysterious began to happen.

Buttonsson continued to laugh, but it sounded as if his laughter were now caught up with some other sound —a strange, wavering hum.

Perhaps it was Strong-tooth. Winter-Hwen always said Strong-tooth would crow after a great battle.

Or perhaps... perhaps it was Cattatoupek.

As the sound grew louder, more shrill and weird, it made Buttonsson's laughter sound more distant—in fact as if it were coming from a long distance away, from the end of a long echoing hall. The wavering sound was now very loud, and now the laughter was coming closer again —though it didn't sound like Buttonsson's laughter any more. It was more like the gurgle and chuckle of a baby.

At the same time the weird noise was growing finer and thinner and more eerie.

And at the same time as that, the darkness of the shippon was alive with another sound—a scuffling and breathing, as if a number of large animals were moving around.

Suddenly everything was silent. Not a sound. Except, from outside, the trudge of heavy boots, and a man whistling gently.

A figure, just visible against Cattatoupek's light outside, appeared in the door of the shippon.

"Myrtle? Maxicrop? Bay 'ee there, you blamed cows?" said Mr Brewer.

At that moment the light, or at any rate some sort of light, began to return.

"My! Yer's a go!" Mr Brewer exclaimed as he

scratched his head in surprise.

This was what Mr Brewer saw.

Directly in front of him, on their hands and knees, were six fat men covered in mud. They looked up at Mr Brewer guiltily and smiled. Then they took off their caps and kneeled up nicely and began to behave themselves.

In front of them were six fat dogs lying good as gold with their noses between their fore-paws. They were grinning and wagging their tails.

In front of them, lying down, were two brown and white cows. They were steaming and sleepily chewing their cud.

And beyond them? It was from somewhere beyond them that the light was coming.

There in the corner of the shippon knelt a girl. Or a woman—it wasn't easy to tell which because the light was so bright it made her features dim and shadowy. Beside her, on the floor, was an old wooden box.

The light, which seemed like one intense cold flame, was coming from the box, or rather from what was in the box—a baby, a gleaming child that lay on its back, laughing and apparently looking up into the face of the woman, or the girl.

Mr Brewer slowly took off his cap, and stood there holding it in both hands.

"Bless us well!" he whispered.

CLATTER-CLANK, came the sound of steel falling onto stone.

What was it that had rattled on the cobbles in front of the child's makeshift cradle?

Had it fallen from the rafters?

Or where?

Mr Brewer stood on tiptoe in his muddied boots to try to see what it was.

What he saw, or what he thought he saw, was this: an old cross-sword, the handle bright with use, and its blade aglow and smoking as if just drawn from the fire.

The light was beginning to fade. The sound of the child's laughter sounded more distant.

Mr Brewer was looking towards the child and the figure of the girl or the woman in astonishment.

As the light grew dimmer, so it was that a new figure began to appear. A tall figure it seemed. A young man, broad-shouldered, who stood at the girl's side.

The light had grown tricky, but it seemed to Mr Brewer that the young man was handsome, and was wearing a brilliant corslet of linked mail. It also seemed that on his head he wore a gold helmet, domed, and with, on either side, a fine curved horn.

But it *was* difficult to tell. Because by now the light had almost gone.

Rustass gave his head a violent shake.

There he was, standing in the starlight outside the cottage. He looked around him in surprise. Why wasn't Buttonsson there. Why, when he had opened his eyes, had he not been looking down into that bright constellation which was Buttonsson's eyes. Perhaps something had gone wrong. He was about to turn and go into the cottage when he heard the sound of light wellingtons out in the lane. Light wellingtons and another sound, sad and threadbare at the edges—the faint, broken sound of Buttonsson singing to himself.

I saw three ships go sailing by
One two three
Three two one
The first ship carried the Moon-on-high

*The second the Summer-sun
But the ship I saw on Christmas Eve
Go sailing by
Over the sea
That ship was carrying the earth and sky
Holly and Ivy and Christmas pie
And you and me.*

Buttonsson closed the gate behind him and started up the path. He appeared to be carrying something which he held hugged to him, half-covered by his denim jacket.

Rustass gave his head another quick shake.

"Where's Puttyboy?" he asked.

"Puttyboy? Who's Puttyboy?"

Rustass bent down and looked closely. He saw that there was something beside stars that glinted in Buttonsson's eyes.

Buttonsson quickly wiped the tears away on one of the sleeves of his denim jacket.

"You're not by any chance," he said, and his voice was a little broken at the edge, "thinking of that ball of old tallow."

Rustass saw the stars blinked away. Buttonsson was smiling.

"Know the answer to the most pointed riddle?" he asked.

Rustass took a deep breath, and looked up at the sky.

"The most pointed..." he began. But stopped. "Hey," he said, "where's Cattatoupek?"

"Cattatoupek?" Buttonsson repeated blankly. "Do you mean that old comet?"

Buttonsson turned and looked down the valley and out to sea.

"There he is," he said. His voice was broken again, scarcely above a whisper. "He's almost gone. Bit of a damp squib, if you ask me."

Rustass narrowed his eyes, and then nodded. He thought maybe he could see, just over the horizon, a small blue light with a tail.

"Gone," Buttonsson said after a while, vaguely. "The ships too. All gone."

"Ships?"

"Yes. You didn't see them? There were three ships."

"Three!" Rustass exclaimed, and he gave the back of his neck an excited scratch with one finger.

"Where did they go?" he asked.

"Good riddle. But I know the answer. South and North and West."

"What sort of ships?"

"I can't do that one. But I *can* tell you how they looked in the moonlight."

"Moonlight?"

Buttonsson grinned for the first time.

"Oh no, I forgot," he said, "there wasn't a moon. Yes there was. There was a silver moon on one of the sails of the Spanish Galleon. That was the one going South. Then the sun was out too. A big red sun that flapped over the heads of the rowers. They were heading North."

"That's two ships," said Rustass.

Buttonsson didn't reply for a moment. When he did speak, it was again with difficulty. There was a crack in his voice.

"I don't know anything about the third ship. Except that it was tall and neat, and shone golden, and sailed West after Catta. . .after that old comet. Straight out to sea."

Buttonsson turned his back on the sea. With his head on one side he looked up at Rustass. Now again Buttonsson's eyes were brimming with stars. But he was smiling.

"I can't think who could have been sailing in the third ship," he said. "Unless perhaps it was the Warrior Child."

Rustass thought for a minute.

"Ah well," he said finally, "there's always Nossno."

"Absolutely," said Buttonsson.

At that moment from inside the cottage came the sound of a large dish being set on the table.

"Funny," they heard Nancy say, her voice full of laughter, "you'd think they'd want their dinner come Christmas Eve. Never mind, I'm hungry enough for three."

"Oh no you don't!" they yelled, and raced for the door.

But before they could reach it, the door had opened.

Rustass and Buttonsson stood side by side on the step. At first glimpse the room seemed to open like a glade in the wood. It had been visited by green vigorous life. The walls were lined with shining holly and glinted with the blood-red berries. The ceiling was hung with dark streamers of ivy. It all appeared alive in the warm moving light of the fire.

The table was laid. The goose was on the table.

"You two look mazed as a couple of moon-men," Nancy laughed. "Come on in before it all gets cold."

Buttonsson gave a deep sigh of content, and came into the room on tiptoe.

"It's beautiful," he said.

Then he went over to Nancy who was standing in

the shadow to one side of the fire.

"And I've got a present for *you*."

"A present? For me? My dear soul!"

"Just an old thing I picked up in the woods," Buttonsson said carelessly. He drew out from under his jacket an odd thing. It looked like the rusted handle of an old cross-sword.

"My!" said Nancy. But as she took it in her hand she said "Ouch!"

"What's the matter?" Buttonsson asked.

"Nothing," said Nancy. "It was just that when I touched it it seemed for a moment so very cold that it burned. But it was only ever a second."

Buttonsson put his head on one side.

"That's right," he said. "That's the answer to the riddle. On Christmas Eve *everything*, even the Bartons, can be changed in a second — in the wink of an eye."

And with that he did wink, and he pointed with a jerk of his thumb over his shoulder to the door.

Rustass was still standing in the doorway. At that moment he chuckled.

"I wonder," he said, "I just wonder what the Bartons are having for their supper."

Buttonsson winked at Nancy again.

"See, what did I tell you?" he whispered. Then he added aloud, "The Bartons? *The* Bartons? I did once know a certain Farmer Barton but...Sssh! Listen!"

The three of them listened. Quite clear they could hear it through the open door. Somewhere nearby one blackbird, full-throated in the dark woods, had begun to carol. Or if not exactly to carol, to sing that rounded song he usually saved for the first evening of spring.

"We'll not crack that one," said Rustass. "That has to be the darkest riddle of all."

But Buttonsson wasn't listening any more. He was looking to the foot of the stairs. No, just to the left, at a Christmas tree. To the base of the Christmas tree. In fact what he was looking at was a shining contraption, a gleaming silver go-cart with at the back an engine, twin red exhausts and broad wheels like those on a racing car.

"Is that for me?" Buttonsson breathed.

"Not till after you've ate your dinner it bayn't," Nancy said. "Blimmin' old invention. Been at it for months, he has. Trust *him* to steal the show."

But as she said it she smiled as if she had been never so happy, and she turned and blew from her fingers Rustass a kiss.

Rustass grinned. He hesitated in the doorway a moment longer. Then with a shrug of his great shoulders he too stepped inside. Behind him the door of the cottage closed on the silent valley, on the crisp starlight, and the frozen worshipping world.

By the same author

Fiction

HEOROT

THE TUGEN AND THE TOOT

Poetry

THUNDER OF GRASS

FIESTA

Highgate
Literary & Scientific
Institution